Praise for *The Green Chamber*

"*The Green Chamber*, [Desjardins's] fifth novel, under a hyperrealistic façade, proposes a completely offbeat, bizarre, and eccentric world." —*La Presse*

∞

"We're familiar with the author of *Maleficium*'s penchant for alternate histories and intrigues in a Victorian atmosphere coloured with Gothic accents ... Isolation, loneliness, extraordinary passions, and cabinets of curiosities ... *The Green Chamber* oscillates between caricatural burlesque and uncanny fantasy." —*Le Devoir*

∞

"Gothic and grotesque, Martine Desjardins's *The Green Chamber* offers a whole gallery of fascinating and complex characters." —*Voir*

∞

Desjardins's previous novels have won a number of awards and prizes, including the 2013 Sunburst Award for Excellence in Canadian Literature of the Fantastic (for *Maleficium*), the 2010 Prix Jacques-Brossard for science fiction and fantasy from Quebec (for *Maleficium*), and the 2001 Governor General's Literary Award for Translation (for *Fairy Ring*, which was translated by Fred A. Reed and David Homel – as have been all of Desjardins's novels to date). *Maleficium* was also a finalist for the 2010 Governor General's Literary Award for French Fiction, the 2010 Prix des libraires du Québec, the 2010 Prix des cinq continents de la francophonie, and the 2010 Prix France-Québec. *All That Glitters* was a finalist for the 2005 Governor General's Literary Award for Translation.

Praise for *Maleficium*

"The collection of confessions takes a deliciously strange approach to remembering and retelling the past. In an unexpected twist near the end, an eighth perspective adds compelling backstory and transports readers to new terrain altogether." — *Quill & Quire*

ॐ

"*Maleficium* is an orgiastic celebration of our five senses ... Drawing on explorers' diaries, medical reference manuals, entomological textbooks, and reference works on the varying professions of those who have confided their secret sins to their parish priest, the novel at the same time impressions the reader with its rigorous attention to detail." — *Le Libraire*

ॐ

"[Martine Desjardins] has dared to write a book unlike any other, dipping her pen in the ink of a bygone day, before nature and its mysteries had been deciphered; when desire loomed with dark and frightening power. The result is an extraordinary festival of the senses." — *Voir*

Praise for *A Covenant of Salt*

"Mining from the past, Desjardins extracts treasures without 'getting caught,' and surfaces like a breath of fresh air. *A Covenant of Salt* marries literary traditions in a sleek gothic ceremony, silvery salt sprinkled like confetti and the Saint Lawrence [River] coursing through."

— *Montreal Review of Books*

The Green Chamber

Also by Martine Desjardins

A Covenant of Salt
All That Glitters
Fairy Ring
Maleficium

All available from Talonbooks

MARTINE DESJARDINS

The Green Chamber

Translated by
Fred A. Reed
and
David Homel

Talonbooks

Talonbooks
278 East First Avenue, Vancouver, British Columbia, Canada V5T 1A6
www.talonbooks.com

First printing: 2018

Typeset in Arno
Printed and bound in Canada on 100% post-consumer recycled paper

Interior design by Typesmith
Cover design and illustration by Cara Bain

Talonbooks acknowledges the financial support of the Canada Council for the Arts, the Government of Canada through the Canada Book Fund, and the Province of British Columbia through the British Columbia Arts Council and the Book Publishing Tax Credit.

This work was originally published in French as *La chambre verte* by Éditions Alto, Montreal, Quebec, in 2016. We acknowledge the financial support of the Government of Canada through the National Translation Program for Book Publishing, an initiative of the *Roadmap for Canada's Official Languages 2013–2018: Education, Immigration, Communities*, for our translation activities.

The author took advantage of this translation to make certain changes to her text.

LIBRARY AND ARCHIVES CANADA CATALOGUING IN PUBLICATION

Desjardins, Martine, 1957–
[Chambre verte. English]
   The green chamber / Martine Desjardins ; translated by Fred A. Reed and David Homel.

Translation of: La chambre verte.
ISBN 978-1-77201-196-8 (SOFTCOVER)

   I. Reed, Fred A., 1939–, translator II. Homel, David, translator III. Title.
IV. Title: Chambre verte. English.

PS8557.E78284C4213 2018   C843'.54   C2018-900690-0

For Lucie, Louis, Élise, Michèle, and Mireille,
in memory of our parents

He that hath ears to hear, let him hear.

—MATTHEW 11:15

PROLOGUE

1964

I knew they would eventually discover the corpse. More conscientious bailiffs would be difficult to find. Had not their eye for detail, bordering on obsession, set them apart as the best among their profession? Even if I had doubted, my fears would have evaporated once I saw them step onto the winding path that leads to my front porch. Rare are those who dare venture into the labyrinth of dead ends, roundabouts, and crescents that describe our little suburb and that, more effectively than the fence that borders our perimeter, protects our secrets from the intrusions of the *vulgum pecus*. Rarer still are those who successfully make their way to my address without having to ask directions of gentlemen out walking their dogs who prefer to feign ignorance rather than become involved in interminable and confusing explanations.

Our street, I admit, is not the easiest to locate, since it is the shortest in the entire Enclave, measuring from one end to the other a single row of dwellings. This infirmity it owes to the obtuse design of our town, which an overly earnest city planner, in his monarchist zeal, laid out along intersecting lines that evoke the design of the British flag. To reach our street, one must first locate either of the two diagonal boulevards and reach the centre without getting lost, turn left just after the post office, cross the bridge that spans the railway line, pass the station and then the rose gardens circumventing the large central park until one comes to the hardware store, turn right just after the pastry shop, and then turn right once more at the first corner onto a street shaded by maple trees. I stand at the extremity of that short avenue, on the south side, on a lot abutting one of the Enclave's six banks – an institution I am often mistaken for because of my distinctive architecture.

Just as certain men are inexplicably fascinated by railways or bridges, Louis-Dollard Delorme, my venerated founder, always had a boundless devotion to banks. His deepest desire was that his private residence rival in appearance the great institutions of Place d'Armes, and he handed the architect whom he had engaged to bring his plans to fruition a detailed list of specifications: on the façade, two elaborately illustrated bronze doors, six Corinthian columns and a tympanum displaying the family coat of arms; at the exact centre of the house, a marbled atrium above which would rise a windowed cupola; in place of an entry, a broad hall lined with teller's windows with a coffered ceiling; and, of course, an armoured vault that could withstand any attempt at theft. The exorbitant costs of construction, however, quickly brought his ambitions crashing to the earth; he was forced to abandon the cupola, the marble and the bronze, and the coffers that were to embellish the ceiling. Of his original project I was able to preserve four columns without capitals on the front porch, a semblance of a crest decorated with a beaver carved from wood, two gilded metal wickets in the entry, a modest transaction counter, and – it goes without saying – the strongroom lodged in the depths of my foundations.

The bailiffs were hardly to be intimidated by so little. How cold-bloodedly they took possession of the place after having broken down my door. They first expelled the three Delorme sisters, who had barricaded themselves in their bedrooms. As they writhed and wriggled, shouting vain threats, the bailiffs seized them and dragged them outside – an easy enough task, since for months the spinsters had been living off tea and Melba toast. Once my premises had been cleared of their encumbering presence, they proceeded to inspect me, and ascertained that I had already been dispossessed of almost all my furniture. They were not hampered by the sixty-seven locks that protected my doors, my cabinets, my drawers, my coffers, and my compartments, and needed only a few hours to carry out a methodical inventory of the vestiges of my past, courageous objects struggling alone against the echoes of rooms now emptied. The empty jar of Postum on the mantelpiece, the Blue Bonnets racing form forgotten between the pages of the telephone directory, the Olivetti calculator, the train transfer slipped into the brim of a hat, the crushed stub of Cuticura soap at the bottom of a laundry hamper, the green metal tackle box, the moth-eaten mouse-fur stole, the rubber gloves left on the edge of the sink, the flask of vanilla extract hidden beneath a mattress, the old rusty picnic table, the calcified cat bones in the garbage incinerator, the morsel of desiccated roast beef behind the radiator, the letter carrier's elastics slipped over the door knobs ... Nothing escaped them.

Having unearthed no objects of value on the first and second floors, they were on tenterhooks as they worked their way down to the basement. Like two wolves on the prowl at the end of a long winter, they rummaged through my entrails with no hesitation, breaking the shackles of padlocks with their hammer blows, and even searching through what had been my coal cellar. So it was that they came upon, tucked in behind the heating-oil tank, the door to the strongroom. Made of armoured steel three inches thick, it had no visible handle, keyhole, or hinges. Not even dynamite could have forced it open. I lent them a hand by activating the opening mechanism, of which I alone here knew the secret. The door swung open on its poorly oiled hinges with the first push. The room exuded the acrid stench of smoke that mingled with the sulphurous fumes of freshly printed banknotes. The bailiffs rushed in, certain to have found at last the legendary reserve where, as rumour had it, the Delormes stashed their fortune.

I

FIRST FLOOR

1963

T he white-gloved finger drew near and, even before it grazed me, I sounded the alarm. The strident peal of my bell pierced the eardrums of my vestibule and caused my entire staircase to vibrate. Clearly, I was crying out in vain. Behind the closed doors of their soundproofed rooms, the Delormes carried on with their activities. What possible reason for concern could they have had? Why should they have had the slightest inkling that the ringing of the bell signalled the beginning of their long, slow decline? Until now, nothing had stood in the way of the rigorous progression of their financial ascent – neither the crash nor the war, nor the upheavals of inflation. During five decades of economic uncertainty, they built their fortune by dint of real-estate speculation, and today were the avaricious proprietors of an apartment building over-looking the park, which assured them a substantial inflow of cash on the first of every month. Whatever made its way into their coffers would never leave as futile expenses. Every cent was counted. And counted again. That, in fact, was their preferred pastime. Every evening after supper, on the green baize of a card table, Louis-Dollard and Estelle would recreate the famous tableau by Flemish painter Quentin Massys, *The Moneylender and His Wife*, as they piled pieces of gold and pearls and cold hard cash upon a small beam balance while Morula, Gastrula, and Blastula, wearing celluloid eyeshades, recorded the sums in the columns of the great ledger. If, by evening's end, the total of credits exceeded that of debits, they would treat themselves to a cup of hot water and some supplementary diversion. On deposit slips purloined from the bank, they entered their name, a fictitious account number, and in the column reserved for the enumeration of bills, a list of amounts according to their inspiration of the moment. These they would then carefully align, taking great pains to accentuate the pleasing contours, and adding feet at the extremities. Then they would duly sign the deposit slips and, in the event the sum passed one million, would dissolve into chortling until they were all but in tears.

Nothing but a powerful explosion could have troubled the calm of such a household. As it was, the young person waiting at my door had, at most, the appearance of a spark – but a spark capable of igniting a conflagration. Without so much as thinking that she might be observed, she bent forward to my letter slot and, lifting the polished brass flap upon which, for a moment, the tip of her freckled nose was reflected, placed her eye against the opening. Between two silky flutterings of her eyelids, she took in the barometer atop the console in the entry hall, the hat stand, and the bouquet of dried immortelles.

The only female visitors we received were the tenants of our apartments – English spinsters with greying hair who affected flannel skirts and flat-soled shoes. Estelle would scrutinize every visitor and, always alert, took pains to ensure they never progressed farther than the entry wicket, where Louis-Dollard, hunched behind the gilded grill, would hand them a receipt for the amount of the rent. As tenants would appear only on the first of the month, the Delormes would open the door to no one the rest of the time for fear of encountering, on the front porch, itinerant vendors, mendicants, or charity ladies soliciting with open hand a few coins for their good works. I should have respected the rule, but the new arrival so awakened my curiosity, and my sympathy, that I could not keep from opening my front door with a welcoming creak.

The young lady stepped into the vestibule and made straight for the office. As she did, she noticed, with a certain indulgence for which I was grateful, the imitation marble stairway, the machine-made carpet, and my fourth-class oak panelling. It was clear that she had a well-trained eye that was not misled by my false opulence. I, who until this very moment, had rarely been exposed to the eyes of strangers, felt myself overcome with indescribable shame. So mortified was I by the inferior quality of my furnishings and materials that my boiler began to overheat; burning water pumped through my galvanized steel veins and rushed into my radiators like blood to a blushing face. Though I rapidly released my valves and opened wide the chimney damper, I reddened right to the eaves. Could the earth have opened beneath my foundations, I would have gladly collapsed then and there. Unfortunately, the clay soil upon which my foundations lie is as stable as the gold standard; my humiliation had only begun.

ಬಌ

"For the apartment to rent, is this where I inquire?"

The young visitor entered the office without knocking and surprised Louis-Dollard in his shirt sleeves, his nose buried in the Blue Bonnets racing form. Since the new clay track opened five years earlier, the names of particular horses would often come trotting through my venerated founder's mind. He imagined himself in white tie and tails, perched on the reviewing stand, tracking the race with his field glasses and clutching his ticket in his fist when the winner brought him twenty times his bet thanks to the advantages of pari-mutuel. Had Estelle any idea of his intemperate proclivities, she would have wrung his neck. Not surprisingly, Louis-Dollard's first reflex was to hide the form spread out before him. But the nameless young woman, with a swift gesture, swept it from his hands.

"You have circled the favourite," she observed as she glanced at the page that described the upcoming races. "Cream Soda has an inflammation of the distal phalanx. I certainly hope you will not bet on him!"

Angered by this unwelcome intrusion, Louis-Dollard got on his high horse and rudely snatched back the form. He was about to show the young lady the door, but at the sight of her youth, her beauty, and her elegance – that print dress, those three strings of pearls, that raffia handbag, those kid gloves! – he thought better of it.

"You seem to know something about horses."

"Think again," she answered. "I can hardly distinguish a stallion from a filly. But I do have a jockey friend who gives me excellent tips, and, according to him, Royal Maple is a sure thing to win next Saturday's derby."

"Royal Maple? Why, he's a very long shot!"

"But he has inherited the exceptional endurance of his father, the great champion Flying Diadem. Over a mile's distance, that certainly counts …"

That was more than enough to calm Louis-Dollard, who adjusted his spectacles and put on his jacket. With clumsy gallantry, for he had never learned proper manners, he drew up the less wobbly of the two mismatched guest chairs and motioned the young lady to sit. He was thoughtful enough to push away a pedestal ashtray from which emanated the pungent stench of cold ashes. Then he returned to his swivel chair and, on the form, drew three circles around the name of the thoroughbred. The thought that, at long last, he could place a bet without fear of losing caused his hand to tremble ever so slightly – all the more so in that he wondered whether or not it was wise to trust a perfect stranger. With a healthy dose of suspicion he turned to her and spoke in his most unctuous voice.

"I did not catch your name, miss."

"Penelope Sterling. But everyone calls me Penny."

"And how might I be of service to you?"

"I am looking to rent an apartment, and the one you are advertising might just do."

"'Might do'!" muttered Louis-Dollard, raising an offended eyebrow halfway up his forehead. "The apartment of which you speak is the most bright and spacious in the entire building. From the bedroom windows one can see the tower of the university and the dome of the oratory. The living room contains a false fireplace, the bathroom is finished entirely in glazed ceramic tile, the walls have recently been repainted, and – it goes without saying – there is a rent to match."

The Delormes were not in the habit of renting to just anyone. Before signing a lease, they required references and guarantees – even if potential tenants appeared to be well heeled.

So it was that Louis-Dollard, displaying precious little consideration, asked her quite directly, "Where are you employed, Miss Sterling?"

Our other tenants hold substantial positions. The Simon sisters, for example, are operators at Bell Telephone. Miss MacLoon works as a translator with Air Canada, Miss Keaton teaches kindergarten at Carlyle Elementary School, and Miss Cressey is a secretary in the finance department at Sun Life. They can be seen every morning leaving the building in grey tailored suits, newspapers in hand, on their way to the railway station to catch the downtown train.

"If by employment you mean receiving a salary, I am sad to disappoint you," answered Miss Sterling. "I have never held a salaried position in my life."

"You are too young to be a widow. You must certainly have family money."

"Saints preserve us! Far from it! I am an orphan, and I assure you I come from an extremely modest background. But I have reached the age of majority, if that is what concerns you. I am fully qualified to sign a contract."

As befits a successful businessman, nothing horrified Louis-Dollard more than wasting time. He gave Miss Sterling his most withering glance and raised the tone of his voice a notch.

"In our building, we insist that the rent be paid in full on the first of every month. If you are unable to meet this requirement, I would prefer to resume my activities."

To demonstrate how deeply he was occupied, he began to strike the keys of his Olivetti Divisumma electromechanical calculator, which shook noisily each time it spat out a result. But Miss Sterling was not to be intimidated. Rummaging through her woven raffia handbag, she withdrew a small booklet and slid it across the desk with a gloved hand. When Louis-Dollard spied the bank book, immediately recognizable by its blue leather cover embossed with silver, the calculator ceased its operations.

"Open it to the last page, if you please," said Miss Sterling.

He did not stop to ask himself if it were improper to commit such an indiscretion; Louis-Dollard needed no convincing. As he turned the pages of the bank book, he noticed that the withdrawal column was all but empty, while that of the deposits, inscribed by the hands of different tellers, presented a series of substantial sums that had all the appearance of a regular source of income. He almost lost hold of his spectacles when his eye came to rest upon the figures that indicated the latest balance: a three followed by four zeros!

"As you can see," said Miss Sterling, "I have more than enough to pay twelve months' rent. And what you see here is but a portion of my assets. The remainder can be found in a safety-deposit box."

Still, Louis-Dollard was not entirely reassured. If Miss Sterling were a kept woman, the other tenants, each of whom religiously attended one or the other of our five churches, would protest indignantly. There would be disorder in the henhouse!

"Such a sum cannot be accumulated in so little time, unless one is involved in shady dealings ..."

Miss Sterling picked up her bank book with a toss of her head.

"I am a discreet individual, Monsieur Delorme, at least with regard to money matters. Nonetheless, I do not wish to mislead you, particularly insofar as I believe I can take you into my confidence. I will reveal the origin of my fortune. Tell me, have you ever heard of the game Safe?"

Louis-Dollard may have been a bit behind the times, but not to the point of being unaware that Safe was the latest parlour-game craze. It was impossible to stop off at the post office or the barbershop without hearing someone talking about it. Whether played alone or with several participants, the principle could not have been simpler. With a roll of the dice, a player advances his piece along a board representing the floor plan of a bank. After crossing the atrium, the wickets, the manager's office, and the safety-deposit-box room, the player reaches the safe, where a small strongbox is located. If, as he advances, the player lands on a red square, an alarm sounds and he loses a turn. If the player stops on a yellow square, he receives a key. Although the game includes ten keys in all, only one will open the safe. The first player to reach it may try his luck. Should he use the right key, he wins the game. Should his key not fit, he must return to square one. Louis-Dollard was familiar with these details. He had also heard that certain people, to lend the game extra excitement, went so far as to wager substantial sums. The bets were deposited in the safe and the winner would lay claim to the contents. How many games could Miss Sterling have won to accumulate thirty thousand dollars, he wondered …

"I do not think it would be appropriate to rent to an inveterate gambler."

"You must understand, I have never made a wager in my life. If this game has proved a source of wealth, it is because I invented it!"

On the insistence of Louis-Dollard, who plied her with questions, she related how the idea had come to her two years before, when she read in the press about a gang of thieves that had taken advantage of Dominion Day to rob the Bank of Nova Scotia via a secret underground tunnel. They were able to enter the vault without setting off the alarm and made off with millions.

"I understood, on that day, that no safe is inviolable, and I began to dream of bank robberies."

She began by drawing up the rules, and then designed the board, the keys, and the pieces. She went on to invent the alarms and locking mechanisms. After applying for a patent, she presented Safe to a prominent toy company based in Massachusetts, which promptly published the game to great acclaim.

"It is hard for me to believe that something so futile could become so lucrative."

"Since I granted the game company a licence without surrendering my rights, I receive 2 percent on each sale," explained Miss Sterling. "So far, more than three hundred thousand sets have been sold, and the orders keep pouring in …"

With a shiver of satisfaction, Louis-Dollard decided at last to open his desk drawer and produce two lease forms. He filled in the blanks, signed each copy, and handed his pen to his new tenant so she could do likewise. Then he walked to the closet and threw open the doors wide. I hoped that, this time, he would spare me the old Bluebeard joke, but as usual, he could not resist.

"Here is where I keep all my wives' keys!"

He handed Miss Sterling five keys on a ring: one for the main entrance, one for the apartment door, one for the letter box, one for the laundry room, and one for the locker. He invited her to move in whenever she wished.

"Before you leave, allow me to ask you one final question. If you are this certain that banks can be so easily robbed, why have you deposited your money in one?"

"To resist the temptation to spend it."

"Such wisdom, at your age, is to your honour."

"Let me assure you: I have no intention of allowing my nest egg to slumber there eternally. I hope to marry one day, and the thirty thousand dollars constitutes a kind of dowry that I will bring as a contribution to the household."

"Far be it from me to cast doubt upon the capacities of the weaker sex in financial matters – my own wife could give lessons to the minister of finance – but a young lady must be cautious, particularly if she is an orphan. In our unscrupulous world, numerous are the men who would not hesitate an instant to abuse your confidence. If ever you feel you need counsel and wish to benefit from my vast experience, my door will always be open. I hope you will look upon me as a friend who seeks only what is best for you."

The unspoken meaning of those words did not escape Miss Sterling, and her expression quickly turned distant. Rather brusquely, she extended her hand to her new landlord without removing her glove.

"Thank you for your kindness, Monsieur Delorme. I will not fail to do so."

As he was getting to his feet to see her to the door, she added, "Do not trouble yourself. I can find my way. And be so kind as to convey my greetings to Madame Delorme. If the redoubtable Estelle is as well informed as you assert, I hope to have the occasion to meet her soon."

Her departure left me in a thoughtful mood. One question in particular bothered me: how did Penny Sterling know the name of our matron, when Louis-Dollard had not once mentioned it in their conversation? She had spoken it, what's more, with a malevolent inflection that should have set off alarm bells in the mind of my venerated founder ... But he already had his nose stuck back in the racing form, and had begun a series of complex calculations designed to ascertain the profit he could make on a winning wager.

The humming and clicking of the electromechanical calculator punctuated the passing hours. When five o'clock sounded, Louis-Dollard quickly concealed the form between the pages of the telephone directory.

"An apartment rented, a lease signed, and a good tenant – and surely not just any tenant: the friend of a jockey who will certainly pass on a tip or two. As the Delormes are my witness, I am far from displeased with the day's work."

Whistling a catchy tune, he wound his way to the living room where Estelle awaited him every afternoon with a richly deserved cup of hot water.

∽

An automobile applied its brakes at the corner – a Rambler Ambassador with chrome trim – and came to an abrupt stop in front of a troop of gentlemen who had just detrained and were rushing home for supper. Two boys on bicycles arrived in the other direction; on a leash they were pulling a cocker spaniel that was barking at squirrels. From her vantage point, adeptly concealed behind the half-open slats of the venetian blinds, Estelle watched their comings and goings while listening to her husband's daily report – in which he took pains to omit any mention of the racetrack. The afternoon light was anything but kind to her fifty-nine years, and accentuated the flaccidity of her flesh. The lower part of her face, made weighty by a flabby double chin, hung over her neck and shook like the wattles of a turkey every time she swallowed. Her hair was the colour of steel wool. Her dull eyes had been reduced to horizontal slits between her puffy eyelids, and grew animated only when Louis-Dollard described the financial situation of their new tenant. With a gurgle of satisfaction, she pulled the cord that closed the blinds and turned toward her husband.

"Yes, indeed," she said. "I believe this joyful event is worth celebrating in fitting fashion."

From the massive ring of keys hanging from her belt, she removed the smallest and made her way toward the mahogany-veneer desk that slumbered in one corner of my living room.

Like the armchairs made of oxblood leather, the pedestal table, and the bronze floor lamps with their corrugated glass shades, this grotesque and tasteless piece had been purchased from Mayor Darling's widow who, facing financial difficulties, was forced to sell her household possessions. The desk contained a secret compartment that Louis-Dollard had had built by a cabinet maker of his confidence. The lock was concealed behind an ornament, and a single turn of the key activated the mechanism that opened the side panel and revealed the hidden compartment. All these precautions to protect a wretched jar of Postum!

Who, since the end of the war, still drank this miserable instant-coffee substitute, whose main ingredients are roasted wheat bran and molasses? Not many people except for Mormons and Seventh-day Adventists, who consume it based on moral conviction. The Postum formula was the invention of the future dry-cereal magnate Charles William Post, who had spent time at Dr. Kellogg's famous sanitarium, where he became convinced of the harmful effects of coffee. But it was not for health benefits that the Delormes made Postum their beverage of choice for grand occasions, but rather for economic ones. A single eight-ounce jar contained seventy-five generous teaspoons of powder, which would yield as many as three hundred cups of ersatz coffee – providing one consumed it parsimoniously. The Delormes' jar, purchased twelve years before, was still half-full. Of course, the Postum it contained had staled somewhat, but neither Louis-Dollard nor Estelle noticed, as they added molasses as a sweetener – the high-green variety, never the fancy grade. In any event, they attached far less importance to the taste of the beverage than the ceremony that accompanied its preparation. As head of the family, Louis-Dollard officiated, standing at the pedestal table. He would measure out the ingredients while uttering a ritual formula of his own invention, which had become, over the years, a near-sacred liturgical dialogue.

"What is that chime?"
"It's Postum time."
"Who shall prepare?"
"Master Delorme with his care."
"What is his secret?"
"Stir six to the right, three to the left, five to the right, two to the left."
"Who knows the secret?"
"The golden globes that keep it."
"And who shall reap the pleasure?"
"The heir to the treasure."

He stirred the mixture as prescribed by the ritual. Estelle offered her hands and received her cup, then paused for a moment of meditation. When she adjusted position to drink, the leather of the cushions squeaked under her weight. Not only had she not maintained her youthful weight, she had doubled it. Her wedding band choked her ring finger, and her slender watchband cut into her fleshy wrist. Her drooping shoulders caused her bosom to retreat to her knees, and the flesh of her ankles was compressed into concentric rings like socks atop her tightly laced shoes. Yet when she stood to speak, she possessed all the aplomb of a general before his subalterns.

"You tell me that this Miss Sterling disposes of a fortune of at least thirty thousand dollars, and that it continues to grow. Do you know how she plans to use it?"

"She makes no effort to hide the fact," replied Louis-Dollard, hypnotized by the swirls of molasses at the bottom of his cup. "It will provide the dowry for her future husband."

With those words, Estelle became so agitated that her mouthful of Postum went down the wrong pipe, and she nearly choked.

"We shall have to change all our plans!"

"What plans?"

"Don't pretend you don't know. I am speaking of Vincent's marriage, of course."

Vincent: their only son, twenty-four years of age, and lawful heir to their estate. He had been promised to Geraldine Knox, the eldest daughter of Charles Knox, the owner of four revenue properties situated on the other side of the park. A match made in heaven, as the saying goes. Except this engagement had been concluded in a dank basement, around a flask of gin, by two fathers who had long dreamed of uniting their fortunes and creating a real-estate empire in the very centre of the Enclave.

Louis-Dollard saw no reason why such excellent plans should be modified, but Estelle, dazzled by the figure of thirty thousand that had begun to glitter before her eyes, reminded him that nothing could beat cash – even bricks and mortar. After all, rental properties, even the most profitable, cost a fortune in upkeep. There are always rooms to be repainted, pipes to be re-soldered, fuses to be replaced, roofs to be re-tarred, masonry to be re-grouted, lawns to be mowed, tiles to be replaced, not to mention property and school taxes to be paid ...

"Just think, Louis-Dollard, of the expense of maintaining Charles Knox's buildings, which are older than ours. If our family takes possession of them, we will never have a peaceful night's rest. If our son weds Penelope Sterling, our greatest concern will be to manage her capital and the revenue it generates. Believe me, we could hardly find a better match for him."

"Vincent can't simply inform Geraldine that he's changed his mind. We could be sued for breach of contract and ordered to pay a substantial indemnity!"

But Estelle had foreseen such an eventuality.

"Don't get in a tizzy. We will simply claim he has had the mumps and would be unable to assure an issue. Charles Knox would never want a sterile son-in-law and would be happy to get rid of him on the cheap."

Louis-Dollard could not withstand his wife's reasoning, especially when she employed that peremptory tone of hers. He knew the price he would pay if he did not demonstrate complete submission. His grand dream of a real-estate empire was turning into dust before his eyes, but rather than abandon it, he tried to stall for time.

"In any case," he pointed out, "it is premature to think of such things. Vincent is at scout camp until the end of the summer."

I can only imagine the impression our valiant leader of the Nickelled Beavers would make on Penny Sterling when he returned from the grand jamboree at Camp Tamaracouta unshaven and sunburnt, a promise pin and merit badges for forest know-how and lifesaving attached to his dirty shirt, wearing his yellow-and-blue kerchief with its Turk's-head knot ... Louis-Dollard may have entertained similar thoughts, for he timidly ventured the opinion that they might need to take Penny's feelings into consideration.

"Unlike Geraldine Knox, she has not yet reached the fateful age of spinsterhood and, given her fortune, she is surely not at a loss for suitors. Why would she fall into the arms of our son who, I might add, is hardly the kind of Lothario the ladies crave?"

A mere detail. Estelle was not troubled in the slightest. She shifted the cups on the pedestal table as though they were pieces on a chessboard, and laid out before her husband the broad outlines of her strategy.

"Vincent need not court her at all. I can quite easily do it for him. I shall organize a reception in honour of Miss Sterling, and there speak of our son so fulsomely she will fall in love with him even before she lays eyes on him."

Invite Penelope Sterling? Here? I could not believe my walls' ears. As far back as I can remember, not a single guest had been invited to our table – and I have an excellent memory. Estelle could not fathom the meaning of the word "guest." At the very most she might have had a vague idea that there existed, elsewhere, among other people, something called society. How could she have hoped to impress a young woman whose sophistication was far greater than she could understand? With a cup of Postum and a spoonful of molasses? Did she think she could amuse her with fake deposit slips to fill out?

Louis-Dollard, who sometimes allowed himself the luxury of reading the society pages of the newspapers, was quick to imagine a grand reception with uniformed chauffeurs and bouquets of hydrangeas, mousse of foie gras and eggs in aspic, chilled champagne and iced petits fours, baskets of Jordan almonds and spun-sugar *pièces montées*, a dance orchestra and tombola tickets. Heavy hearted, he began pacing back and forth, his arms describing great windmill motions.

"By our queen, Elizabeth II, that will drive us into poverty!"

"Calm down," his wife replied. "Can't you see you're wearing out the carpet? And stop taking Her Majesty's name in vain! Before we incur any needless expenses, we will dispatch you to investigate Miss Sterling, and your three sisters will be assigned to probe her preferences. That way we won't purchase roses should she prefer wildflowers ..."

Louis-Dollard stopped in front of the fireplace, resigned but not reassured.

"So be it," he said. "I hope we will not have cause for regret. How much do you estimate this seduction will set us back?"

"One hundred dollars or so. I know, it's an indecent sum, but we will have recovered it within the year. And imagine the profit we will have made on our initial investment!"

"Petty cash will not be enough," said Louis-Dollard in a voice that trembled into a squeaky whisper. "We will have to withdraw funds from the Treasury ..."

Under my roof, no one uttered the word "Treasury" without sensing he had violated a taboo. It was such a well-protected secret that I myself often forgot I was its designated custodian. The Treasury had always been hidden deep within me, in a void where light, which would reveal its true nature, never entered. I had begun to think, over the years, that its muffled echoes in that darkness were the sounds of my own heart beating. A heart of gold, of course, as golden as silence. A closed heart, numbed by forgetfulness and enfeebled by years of neglect, a heart that must continually contain its overflow. For I am rich with the disillusionment and disappointment that have been my lot. I seethe with resentment toward the Delormes, who have left me dressed in rags while a tiny portion of that Treasury of theirs would have made me new again …

Estelle had to overcome her reticence before finally nodding in agreement. My venerated founder rose to his feet and, with heavy footfalls, moved toward the mantelpiece where a clock stood, alone – the only reminder we retained of Oscar Delorme, Louis-Dollard's brother, who was a watchmaker. It was one of those glass-domed German marvels known as anniversary clocks, so called because they require winding only once a year. Instead of oscillating, their mechanism is driven by a torsion pendulum that, with a minimal loss of energy, turns a balance wheel mounted with four golden balls. Not quite perpetual motion, but almost. We owe this splendid invention to a certain Anton Harder, who drew his inspiration from the rotation of a chandelier in a draft of air. Complicated to wind, prone to malfunction if its base is not perfectly motionless, the anniversary clock is not very accurate; the slightest shift in temperature changes the tension of the spring and makes it gain or lose time.

Our particular anniversary clock, on whose face was inscribed the motto Time Is Money, had long ceased to function. That did not keep Louis-Dollard from lifting the glass dome and rotating the gilded balls of the balance wheel – six turns to the right, three to the left, five turns to the right, two to the left. When he finished, Estelle joined him in front of the fireplace.

"We are about to commit a grave sin," she said sanctimoniously. "We must confess without delay. Go summon your sisters. We must all go down to the Green Chamber and seek absolution from Her Majesty."

1913

They came like thieves in the night. Forty men from the Canadian Northern Railway Company dressed in black, from their felt hats to their polished boots, holding identical grey paperboard binders under their arms. Their watches were synchronized to the second and, at the stroke of eight o'clock, they knocked simultaneously at the doors of the forty farms scattered across the territory of Côte Saint-Laurent, to the north of Mount Royal. The farmers were about to go off to bed, but their wariness was already asleep. Misled by the strangers' formal attire and appearance of respectability, they showed them in and put on water to boil for tea.

Even before filling their pipes, the agents launched into an explanation of the reason for their visit. Speaking at locomotive speed and in the most sombre tones, they had come to announce the end of rural life as people knew it. Thanks to the latest chemical fertilizers that increased multifold the production of the fields, and the mighty machines that harvested their crops without effort, great agricultural enterprises could now feed an entire city with the production of a single farm. Equipped with huge trucks to transport this agricultural manna, foods from such farms would soon flood the markets of Montreal, offering products at prices so paltry that small farmers would never be able to compete. Within a year, the value of the land around the city would be reduced to next to nothing. They should sell while there was still time.

The farmers were devastated. Their wives began to weep, their children as well. That was when the agents opened their binders and withdrew long sheets of paper covered in fine print. By providential coincidence, they explained, Canadian Northern was planning to build a railway line in the immediate vicinity. If the families agreed to forsake their farms before springtime, the company was prepared to pay them ten dollars an acre – a more than fair price, considering the circumstances. But they would have to make up their minds without delay; to avoid an outbreak of unbridled speculation, this exceptional offer expired at midnight and would not be repeated. Terrified at the thought of being the only holdouts in the area, thirty-nine farmers signed the contracts of sale on the spot. The fortieth, clever to a fault, decided to wait and see.

ന്ധ

With his four hundred acres of fertile fields, Prosper Delorme was the largest landowner in the area, though he did not advertise it. He wore the same oft-patched shirt he had worn since his wife died in childbirth three years before, leaving him to care for two young sons and three daughters. There were holes in the soles of his boots. His house had never been repainted, and the windows were patched with rags and newspaper. The crusty farmer was hardly a model of hospitality. He left the Canadian Northern agent shivering on the doorstep before finally letting him in. And though he allowed him in the house, he did not ask him to sit and certainly did not offer a cup of tea.

With the exception of the faint halo of light from the vacillating flame of a kerosene lamp, the house was in darkness, and the agent could barely make out the faces of the children who watched him with wary eyes, their heads thrust between the balusters of the staircase like five birds in a cage.

Prosper let him recite his routine to the end, then answered with a resounding, "I can't hear a thing."

True enough, he was a bit hard of hearing. But he took perverse pleasure in exaggerating his deafness to trump his adversaries or rid himself of unwanted guests. The agent finally realized it was useless to shout at Prosper; he would have to find another way of making himself understood. In frustration, he laid on the table the document that his superiors had expressly forbidden him to show the sellers for any reason. The widower was a sly fox. At first glance he understood exactly what the project staring him in the face involved.

It was not a simple railway line that was to be built, but an entire urban development to be named Model City, conceived and designed by Frederick Gage Todd, a landscape architect of renown, based on recent garden city designs in the suburbs of New York, Pittsburgh, and Boston. The founders of the Canadian Northern Railway wished the city plan, with its two diagonal arteries, to symbolize the Union Jack; however, its spokes linked by broken concentric circles reminded the observer more of a spider's web with, instead of dewdrops, thirty-six circular and oval parks. All the essential features of a city had been planned: a city hall, police station, fire house, a library for adults and another for children, a recreation centre, an outdoor swimming pool, two indoor rinks for hockey and curling, golf courses, tennis and lawn-bowling clubs, baseball fields, churches of various denominations, schools, banks, a shopping district, an electric-power substation, and, last but not least, a railway station, which would be the focal point of the entire scheme.

Prosper Delorme could indeed rub his hands together when he set eyes upon the plan: the location of the future railway station coincided exactly with that of his melon patch! Without his signature, the entire venture would collapse. The very future of the railway company depended upon the success of the project. At the time, Canadian Northern was a small player in the struggle for control of transcontinental rail transport. Though its network extended from Quebec City to the West, it had no access to the centre of Montreal, as all the approaches were occupied by the tracks of its powerful rivals, Canadian Pacific and Grand Trunk. There was a possible northerly entrance, but it was blocked by Mount Royal – a major obstacle, for its slopes were far too steep to lay tracks.

Driven by the vital necessity of expansion, the company's founder, Sir Donald Mann, had entrusted the problem to his right-hand man, chief engineer Henry Wicksteed. The latter proposed a solution that Mann first judged to be wildly impractical: digging a tunnel under Mount Royal, an overall length of three miles. It was not the scale of the would-be passage that concerned him (tunnels four times longer had been dug through the Alps), but its price, which he calculated at no less than three million dollars.

Wicksteed then played his ace: the financial arrangement that would ensure recovery of the initial investment in less than three years. The company simply needed to acquire at low cost the agricultural lands that lay north of Mount Royal, then transform them into a residential zone and sell the lots at a handsome profit when the proximity of the railway had increased their value. The cost of operating the new line would be entirely financed by new suburbanites who would purchase tickets every day to travel into the city. The transaction, which would involve 4,800 acres of land, would be the most spectacular in the history of Montreal real estate – and it would cost Canadian Northern the modest sum of forty-eight thousand dollars.

Their calculations failed to take into account the cunning of Prosper Delorme. He put the company agent on notice that he would accept nothing less than two hundred dollars an acre. And since he had warned that he might well offer his land to Canadian Pacific, Mann was forced to involve himself directly.

Having built railway lines in faraway places, including Brazil and China, the magnate was confident that his powers of persuasion would prevail when he presented himself early one morning at the widower's house. But Prosper was ready for him. He rejected every offer made and would not listen to reason. At the end of long hours of negotiation, he had yielded no more than 5 percent, and had won an important concession: he would retain ownership of his house and the land on which it was built.

Before losing what little face he had left, Mann signed the promise of sale. The transaction, which should have amounted to four thousand dollars, had cost him seventy-two thousand more. As he left, he turned and spoke to the widower's children – Louis-Dollard, Oscar, Morula, Gastrula, and Blastula – who were standing neatly in a line on the front porch.

"Your father drives a hard bargain," he said. "Learn from what you have seen. And never forget to say a prayer for this blessed day when your family made its fortune."

ಬಬ

Clearly, it was out of question for Prosper to keep such a sum in his root cellar, where he normally hid his savings. As soon as he received the cheque, he hastened to open an account at the head office of the country's largest bank. To further his son's education, he dressed Louis-Dollard in his Sunday best and brought him along.

The bank was located in a monumental building crowned with a dome modelled on the Roman Pantheon, an edifice that loomed over Place d'Armes. Deeply impressed by the six Corinthian columns that lined its portico, Louis-Dollard stepped back to admire the façade graced with an illustrated tympanum whose coat of arms, resting atop a horn of plenty, was flanked by two Indians and various symbols of commerce and industry.

"You enter a bank the way you enter a church," his father

whispered as a security guard wearing a top hat and greatcoat opened the bronze doors. "Don't say a word, just follow me."

Prosper had no sooner crossed the threshold than a sudden gust of wind powerful enough to knock a man off his feet swept him into the lobby. He strode through the atrium and, as he came into the great room with its rows of wickets, he noticed a change in the sound of his footsteps on the marble floor, which he attributed to the dizzying height of the coffered ceilings, and the reverential silence that reigned there, interrupted from time to time by the swish of banknotes in the dextrous hands of those who were counting them out. There could be no doubt about it: he was in a cathedral – a cathedral where the odour of money had supplanted that of incense, and where wickets had taken the place of confessionals. Here, there was no statue of the Virgin, but of Britannia, she of placid gaze. No altar, but a docket counter. No crucifix either, but a life-sized portrait of good King George V. Prosper advanced respectfully, and as he came to a halt beneath the portrait, he felt an electrical current coursing through him. Irrepressible, the wave caused the ancient coin that he always kept on his person to vibrate, producing a jingling sound that echoed beneath the lofty cupola.

Prosper held his breath. No doubt about it, he was in the presence of an unknown power capable of attracting money and commanding the fortunes of men. He even began to suspect that His Majesty was the focus of a secret cult, whose most devout followers – bankers, financiers, and captains of industry – benefitted from his protection and generosity. He could hardly believe that, until now, he had been ignorant of the existence of this Supreme Being, and he was almost inspired to remove his shoes out of respect, like Moses before the burning bush. He collected his thoughts a moment, then took a solemn oath to dedicate a sanctuary to Him so that he might reside among his people. If, as the Gospel says, one cannot serve both God and Mammon, he would sell his soul to His Majesty and never set foot in a church again. The days when he paid his tithe and dropped money in the collection plate were well and truly over.

A teller standing behind his gilded wicket beckoned Prosper to advance and looked over at Louis-Dollard.

"It is never too soon to instill in one's children the importance of saving," he said, adjusting his spectacles. "Are we to open an account for the lad as well?"

Urged on by his father, Louis-Dollard enunciated his name and address. In return, he received a blue-covered bank book in which were inscribed an account number and his bank balance. For the moment, it stood at one cent, but the value of that cent would increase one hundredfold, as would all that he deposited here, the teller assured him. Louis-Dollard could hardly believe his ears.

He was so enchanted by his visit that he promised his father as they left, "I shall own a bank when I grow up."

ന്ദ

On returning to the farmhouse, Prosper checked his traps. He had snared five rabbits, which he skinned. He left their skins to macerate overnight in a lime solution, then simmered them until they disintegrated. From the kettle he was able to extract a thick glue that he applied to the roof of the cellar. Then he went to the shelf where he kept jars of pennies hidden behind pots of jam. There he chose the brightest copper coins and set to work. He may not have had the talents of the master mosaic artists who gilded the domes of Constantinople, Venice, and Ravenna, but his work was painstaking and thorough, and after several weeks the cellar ceiling was lined with gleaming tesserae, reflecting the light of the lamp in myriad facets, like the compound eye of a fly. Each coin had been glued with the sovereign's head displayed, to the greater glory of His Majesty.

Once Prosper had completed his work, he roused his sons,

Louis-Dollard and Oscar, as well as his daughters, Morula, Gastrula, and Blastula, and led them down to the cellar so they might admire his work. The children, still in their nightshirts, were so dazzled by the constellation of shiny copper coins that they fell to their knees on the damp earthen floor and intertwined their pudgy fingers.

"From now on, this is the place where we will come to pray, take communion, confess our sins, and offer our devotions," said Prosper. "It will be the holy place of our new religion."

Then he took from his coin purse five coins, which he blessed in "the name of Capital, Interest, and the Holy Economy," sketching in the air, instead of the sign of the Cross, the symbol of the Canadian dollar: a capital *S* intersected by a parallel vertical line. He then laid the coins on the outstretched tongues of the children as though they were the Holy Spirit, warning them not to swallow. Too late for Louis-Dollard: the penny was already in his gullet.

"Give thanks to His Majesty," the father instructed his sons. "By his grace, you will never have to work the land. You will become wealthy businessmen."

"And us? What about us?" asked his daughters. "Will we be rich one day?"

Prosper looked at them, eyes welling with pity.

"You? You will be the sacrificial lambs."

❧

It was not long before work began on the new Model City, and Prosper Delorme had a front-row seat to observe the town take shape. Every morning, he began his rounds at the foot of Mount Royal, where a legion of Italian labourers was hard at work digging the tunnel, armed only with picks and shovels. For many long years, these recently arrived immigrants had excavated marble from the quarries of Tuscany and Liguria, and a little sedimentary rock was not about to stop them. They were divided into two teams assigned to each end of the tunnel, and they moved toward each other at the rate of 420 feet per month. At first, horses hauled the carts filled with fragmented gabbro and diorite, but once the first rails were laid, gasoline-powered locomotives were pressed into service, despite the asphyxiating fumes they spat out. The two teams finally met in December 1913 (eighteen months after the project was initiated), 620 feet below ground. So precise were chief engineer Wicksteed's calculations that where the two tunnels joined, the misalignment amounted to one inch on the horizontal axis and a quarter-inch on the vertical.

As ill luck would have it, such an excellent beginning was soon cut short by the entry of the country into war, and for the next four years, Prosper Delorme had little in the way of spectacle with which to regale himself. The army had requisitioned all raw materials, and fortification of the tunnel walls with concrete, which brought the overall cost to five million dollars, was not completed until December 1916. Of the some seven thousand residential lots offered for sale to finance the railway line, only twenty or so found buyers. Crushed by debt, Canadian Northern was forced to suspend laying tracks and installing the catenary until further notice. A Royal Commission of Inquiry was set up, which recommended that the government purchase Canadian Northern's shares and merge its activities with those of its own railway company to create a transportation system that would serve the country's harbours from one sea to the other. And so the fiasco of our town was the founding moment in the nation-alization of the transcontinental railway.

On the morning of October 21, 1918, the first train, drawing six coaches, left Central Station and made its way through the tunnel in the direction of Model City. If not a puff of steam issued from locomotive number 601, it was because the engine was a General Electric Z-1-a Boxcab – the same type used in

1963

Louis-Dollard hardly had time to take off his hat before Estelle ripped it from his hands and tossed it onto the hat stand in the hallway. In short order she led her husband into the dining room, where the settings were placed on a vinyl lace tablecloth, and closed the sliding doors behind her.

"So?" she whispered, in such a low voice I had to read her lips to understand. "What did you find out?"

This was her favourite moment of the day. Her husband, returned from his daily rounds of the apartment building, would report what he had heard in the hallways, what the janitor had gossiped about, and, above all, what had come of his personal inquiries. He had been only half-joking when he told Penelope Sterling that the keys to the apartments belonged to his wives: his tenants held no secrets. He had no scruples about entering while they were out and rummaging through their drawers, closets, even their medicine chests. He took the greatest care to put everything back exactly where he found it, and the tenants suspected nothing.

And so it was that Louis-Dollard discovered certain preposterous compulsions, certain occasionally scabrous eccentricities, the divulging of which during the evening meal would bring his family hours of good-humoured diversion. Beatrice Cressey, for example, owned at least a hundred pairs of gloves in every imaginable colour and she never wore the same pair two days in a row. They filled an entire chest of drawers and were promptly replaced at the slightest sign of wear. The Harris sisters were chain-smokers, and the walls of their apartment were covered with a nicotine slime that, in certain places, oozed down in long yellowish smears. Jeanne MacLoon had been knitting the same scarf for more than eighty-three months and appeared no closer to completion, for she finished only one row a week. Florence Hill had brought back from Seville a tortoiseshell comb and a mantilla with which she embellished herself when she prepared Spanish rice. Elderly Madame Sainte-Marie was so terrified her transistor radio would catch fire that she stored it in the freezer when she finished listening to the live Metropolitan Opera broadcast on Saturday afternoons. Liliane Hannah, who was of Lebanese origin, covered her walls with gilt-framed mirrors upon which she wrote in nail polish, "With my reflection, I am never alone." Mona Partridge would spend hours on the telephone and, as she spoke, would draw phalluses in a small stapled notebook; they took on fantastic forms that had little to do with nature, which could possibly be explained by the fact that the artist was a case-hardened virgin. Mervine Lennard, who refused to divulge her origins, subscribed to a German periodical printed in Gothic script, and claimed to have killed the zebra whose hide graced the floor of her living room. Madame Agababa imported from Turkey cases of rose and pistachio lokum, which she served her guests claiming it was homemade. Susan Keaton had a collection of dolls for which she spent a fortune in hats and dresses, and if one of them dirtied her clothes, she would shave her head in punishment. Over the years, Louis-Dollard learned to draw certain conclusions from his observations. In his opinion, blue-eyed women's pantries were empty; brunettes made their beds every morning, but neglected to wash the floors; widows could not live without bouquets of artificial flowers that they, in their confusion, insisted on watering; and the ones who wore glasses frequently lost their keys …

Today, a new tenant's name was added to Louis-Dollard's

tally: Penny Sterling, and Estelle felt a curiosity so overwhelming about her that her voice turned hoarse and her gaze hollow. Her husband, meanwhile, sat down in leisurely fashion at the head of the table and brushed back with the palm of his hand the few hairs that covered his baldpate. He opened his napkin and tied it around his neck. His movements were more deliberate than necessary. He had not yet accepted that his alliance with Mr. Knox was foiled, and took obvious pleasure in seeing his wife roasting over a slow fire. They had been married for twenty-six years now, and though the foundations of their partnership were as solid as ever, each of them had accumulated small resentments, minor annoyances, that would rise to the surface at such moments, calling for prompt retribution.

It was clear to Estelle that Louis-Dollard would not speak until his meal was served. Resigned, she banged on the dinner bell, knowing her sisters-in-law were never eager to come and eat. Morula was the first to appear. She emerged from the laundry room where, in between washing, ironing, and sewing, between darning socks, mending dish towels, and re-looping threads of the terrycloth towels, she found time to read romance novels in secret. Behind the fogged lenses of her glasses, her eyes were moist from tears. Then came Blastula, wearing her customary black trousers and white cotton-jersey turtleneck. With her crepe-soled shoes, she walked soundlessly. If my floorboards did not deliberately creak beneath her feet, no one would have heard her approach. She had spent the entire morning disinfecting the bathroom taps, and chlorine bleach had corroded her fingers. Last but not least, Gastrula brought the soup. She had gotten even thinner, and her hair, close-cropped with fingernail scissors, did little to frame her fleshless face. Though she was in charge of the kitchen, food was not one of her priorities. If she could have, she would have gladly done without, and subsisted instead on concentrates in tubes, like the cosmonaut Yuri Gagarin in his space capsule *Vostok 1*.

37

All three were in their late fifties, and time had acted upon them as it does on dead leaves, drying up the little freshness of their green years that remained. Their lips were so chapped they split at the slightest hint of a smile – something that happened with exceeding rarity. For more than twenty-five years now they had been treated like poor relations, toiling under the thumb of their sister-in-law, obeying her innumerable rules and regulations to the letter. Why should they take any pleasure in being conscripted into her latest undertaking? They could not have cared less about their nephew Vincent's eventual marriage with someone they had only heard speak of, wealthy though she might be, and even less of the arrival of an heir, which could signify for them only a setback in the order of succession, which for the Delormes was determined by the rule of male primogeniture. So they folded their arms and put on their most sullen expressions when Estelle raised the subject of the new tenant with their brother.

"Tell us at least if her decor is as comely as her dress suggests."

Louis-Dollard took his time. He adjusted his napkin and waited until Gastrula had served the vermicelli soup before answering.

"Clothes do not necessarily make the man, my dear, for Penelope Sterling lives in a state of near-total privation. Her furnishings are limited to the barest necessities: nothing but a bed, a chest of drawers, a table, a chair, and an armchair.

"How is the apartment decorated?"

"No paintings on the walls, no rugs on the floor, no drapes on the windows. And none of those feminine knick-knacks that gather dust."

He crushed three saltines into his soup and hastened to slurp it down before it cooled off.

"What did you find in her pantry?"

"The basics. Marmalade. Nutmeg. Tapioca. Vanilla extract. Several cakes of maple sugar."

"And in her medicine chest?"

"Nothing but a bottle of Aspirin."

Estelle nodded in approval. There were three pharmacies in the centre of the Enclave, and she could not understand why people insisted on spending a fortune on medications when, at the Delormes', they made do quite nicely without. Be it a sore throat, an infected wound, a toothache, or a burn, they used the same tried-and-true remedy: a spoonful of pickling salt dissolved in a glass of hot water. Soon enough they would be in fine fettle.

"Did you go through her drawers?"

"Obviously. I did not see much clothing, but what I did see was of irreproachable quality. Perfumed sachets deposited among silk stockings. And extremely modest nightdresses," he added, coughing to conceal his embarrassment. "Hmm! Hmm! Did you say there was some tea left?"

"That's all?" Estelle burst out in vexation.

"I would have a half-banana with corn syrup," answered Louis-Dollard.

"Stop acting innocent. You're not going to tell me you spent two hours in Miss Sterling's apartment and didn't find the bait that will lure her into our nets!"

It was clear that he still had an item or two in his bag of tricks, and since he intended to take maximum advantage, she could only capitulate. Spitefully she ordered Gastrula to serve dessert.

Louis-Dollard feigned reflection, calculated his effect, and declared in an accusatory tone, as though he were delivering a piece of incriminating evidence, "There was a tennis racket in the vestibule closet!"

The spinsters had heard enough. With disdainful pouts they rose from the table, but Estelle motioned them to sit back down. She now wore her master strategist's expression, which she adopted when she assigned them their weekly tasks. What plot was she hatching?

"I have a plan!" she announced, speaking to Morula. "You've been dreaming about tennis for a long time, and this is your chance! Tomorrow, you will register at the Enclave's private tennis club. You will invite Penelope Sterling, and between sets, you will tease out what she's hiding."

It would be fair to say that the eldest of the three sisters had developed a marked interested in tennis. She even took old sugar sacks and fashioned a pleated skirt modelled on the one worn by the young champion Margaret Smith when she won the French Open, the Australian Open, and the United States Open. Attired all in white according to the prevailing dress code, she strode through Connaught Park to the courts. But contrary to what Estelle thought, she had no desire to play the sport or even follow, as a spectator, the balls being volleyed over the net.

I know why she hung around the tennis club. Our Morula, despite having reached a certain age, had lost none of her romantic and impressionable nature: she hoped to meet a man. But not just any man. The suntanned coaches and the shorts-clad players drinking iced tea at the outdoor tables left her cold. From behind her round glasses with the black plastic frames, she had eyes only for the squad of Italian groundskeepers who trimmed the cedar hedges, watered the rose bushes, and mowed the lawns. She was fascinated by the sweat running down their swarthy skin, the swelling muscles that stood out beneath their damp undershirts, and, most of all, their soil-blackened fingernails. She imagined those nails digging into the flesh of her thighs; that alone was enough to cause her to swoon.

From the bushes of the rose garden, Morula could observe the workers at her leisure. Sometimes she would tear off a few petals, bite into them just enough to leave the imprint of her crooked incisors, then leave them strewn on the paths where the men, in their muddy boots, would be likely to pass. At the end of the day, she would take up position by the fence of the lawn-bowling green in hopes of being noticed. But the gardeners were in too much of a hurry to catch the tram that would take them back to their wives and families in the poor districts where immigrants lived. And Morula would make her way home, scuffing her tennis shoes, once she'd beheaded with a swipe of her hand those unfortunate roses that found themselves in her way.

To become a member of a club is one thing. To indulge in a sport of which one knows neither the rules nor the rudiments is something else. Lacking flexibility, strength, and balance, Morula never showed the slightest aptitude for physical activity of any kind. Even as a little girl, she failed her backflips and kept entangling her feet in her jump rope. When someone threw a ball at her, she was so frightened of being hit she closed her eyes and froze instead of trying to catch it. She started riding a bicycle well after her younger sisters and never learned to swim. Since she had never set foot on a tennis court, I would have been very surprised had she mastered the backhand or the drive overnight.

When Morula grew despondent about her performance, Estelle attempted to reassure her.

"You'll manage just fine. Hitting a ball shouldn't be more difficult than beating a carpet."

"But I don't even have a racket!"

"Louis-Dollard will give you money and you can buy one at Modelectric. It's the perfect time. This week their merchandise is 30 percent off."

Modelectric was the neighbourhood hardware store. Beside paint, tools, and metalworking supplies, it sold sporting goods, television sets, Christmas ornaments, and household appliances. The Delormes had been faithful customers ever since it opened in 1953 – the very year a portrait of Her Majesty Elizabeth II surrounded by a wreath of roses to celebrate the coronation had been placed in the shop window. That week, the hardware store was holding a liquidation sale, since it would be moving to the shopping centre that would soon be opening on the other side of the railway tracks.

If Morula could bring down the price of the racket, she would have enough money left over to indulge in her secret vice. It wouldn't be the first time she was guilty of embezzlement. As we so well know, nothing can be more costly than a bad habit.

203

Morula was practising her strokes against the garage door, causing an infernal racket every time the ball struck the sheet metal that covered the rotting wood. Fortunately, the exercise did not last long. After ten minutes or so, she looked around to make sure no one was watching, and before being caught in the act, she snuck into the garage.

Once her eyes were used to the darkness, and her nose to the potent stench of motor oil that saturated the air, she slipped between the concrete wall and the muddy fenders of the car, taking great care not to soil her white skirt. She stopped to look at herself in the side-view mirror. She made a face. I couldn't blame her: she was hardly at her best with her tired features and clouded complexion. Today was the day she would make her debut at the tennis club, and naturally she wanted to look her best.

She moved to the back of the garage, where Louis-Dollard had his workbench. Made of hemlock, the table had been smoothed by constant use and scarred by the bite of tools. Awls, handsaws, hammers, planes, and drills hung from a panel of fibreboard on the wall behind it, displayed like a collection of weapons. Morula went to the shelf where cans of paint and stripper were lined up in order. She shoved aside the perfectly classified jars of screws and spotted an old jam pot filled with leftover bits of metal. Removing the lid, she fumbled through the metal scraps, shook the pot impatiently, and finally emptied it out on the workbench. At last she found what she was looking for: a rusty bolt of considerable size. Clamping it between the jaws of the vise, she rubbed it with an emery board until the iron gleamed.

I did not understand at first what she was trying to achieve, but I began to suspect when I saw her place the tiny particles of rust in the palm of her hand and add a dollop of hinge grease. Dipping her index finger into the mixture, she applied it to her cheeks in broad circular movements, and then smeared it thickly on her lips.

"Don't I look like a real doll!" she said, satisfied, to her reflection in the side-view mirror.

Why stop there? She lent herself a mysterious air by dusting her eyelids with a cloud of soot, and tried to curl her eyelashes with needle-nose pliers. On the shelf she located the dregs of some mahogany-tone wood varnish and applied it to her fingernails. Only the final touch was missing: a drop or two of turpentine behind her ears and on the insides of her wrists – just enough to envelop her in a camphoric mist. It was eleven o'clock, and Penelope Sterling was waiting for her at the tennis club.

ოა

A throng of the curious had gathered around the court where Penny and Morula made their entrance. New members of the club were always welcomed with ceremony, and from here I heard the sound of applause. Penny immediately took up position on the baseline, while Morula kept her eyes glued on the chain-link fence. Twisting the hem of her pleated skirt, she watched one of the groundskeepers watering the flowerbeds. The man had taken off his shirt and tied it around his waist. Square of shoulder and jaw, a thick black moustache fell over his lips and partially covered his mouth, from which a tooth was missing. I have no idea whether Morula was attracted to or repelled by the dark gap, but she applauded foolishly when the groundskeeper, through the interstice, discharged a stream of sputum as vigorous as the water spraying from his hose.

The first set got underway at last, and from my observation post, I watched the match unfold through the foliage of the

majestic elms. At first, Penny displayed great courtesy. She had a
strong service, but, fortunately, it turned out, she refrained from
using her full strength. Though she directed the ball straight
at Morula, the latter could not return a single serve – perhaps
because, instead of focusing on the incoming projectile, she
tried to attract the attention of the groundskeeper, who went
on watering the flowers with his back turned. She could not
execute a backhand, much less so a volley. As for her service –
my word! – I would rather remain silent. Their exchanges were
brief, and before ten minutes elapsed, the match had ended.

Soundly thrashed, Morula was in such a hurry to leave the
court that she forgot to congratulate her opponent on her vic-
tory. Emboldened by the mask of her makeup, her only thought
was to rush over to the groundskeeper, who was busy weeding
a bed of peonies in the park. She wanted to surprise him, and
crept up behind him on tiptoe. It was then that an unfortunate
incident occurred. Just as she came up beside him, he turned
his head and let fly a gob of spit that hit her square in the eye.
The frothy expectorate hung for a moment from her eyelashes
before slipping down her cheek in a swale of rust and soot.
The groundskeeper was a rather primitive sort. He mumbled
excuses in his incomprehensible patois and walked away, rolling
his shoulders.

Morula had never felt so humiliated. She tried to wipe her
face with her sleeve, but managed only to spread the smear.
Around her, general hilarity broke out. Children were pointing
at her and even I could not keep from laughing at her grotesque
appearance. Only Penny was charitable enough to rush to her
defence. She handed her the hanky she had moistened in the
water fountain and helped cleanse her face with a kindness that
Morula, in her distress, was unable to appreciate.

"There, there, Mademoiselle Delorme. Everything will be
fine, you need not worry. It was so kind of you to invite me
today, and I hope you will allow me the pleasure of returning

the favour. Will you join me at the opening of the shopping centre next Saturday? The women's wear shops are organizing a show to present their summer fashions, and they asked me to participate as a model. There will be a merry-go-round for the children and door prizes. We could even arrange to lunch together, if you like ..."

Morula returned the hanky with a wary look. Caught off guard by a sign of friendship she was not accustomed to, she wondered if Penny was making fun of her.

"Give me a few days to think about it," she replied, taking pains not to commit herself, though rarely had any invitation been more tempting.

෴

Morula squatted down in the darkest corner of her room. With her paint-stained fingernails, she lifted one of the slats of my parquet. The secret space was just large enough to hold a two-liquid-ounce amber vial with a faded, barely legible label that read, "Burnett's Pure Vanilla Extract – The Essence of Economy." Made in Boston, this extract was produced by distilling the beans of the vanilla orchid, and it contained 35 percent clear alcohol as per the recipe of Joseph Burnett, the pharmacist who made his name providing ether for the first dental anaesthetic and who, in 1847, at the request of an aristocratic French woman, invented a process for the extraction, in liquid form, of vanilla aroma – a process he later applied to more than twenty-five other aromatics, including nutmeg, celery, banana, and violet. Whoever tasted this essence experienced ethylic euphoria, a feeling of vertigo and exaltation that quickly led to physical dependence.

Morula, who tried to abuse vanilla in moderation, reserved it for grand occasions. But today she removed the cork and brought the bottle to her lips, tilted her head as far back as her cervical vertebrae would allow, and gulped down the contents.

The alcoholized extract burned her tongue, her throat, and her chest as its warmth slowly radiated through her body, promising a calming effect. Morula closed her eyes and waited for her swollen heart to stop tormenting her – without for a moment thinking of the door, which she had forgotten to lock.

Estelle, meanwhile, had heard her come in, and in her eagerness to find out what had happened, chose that moment to burst into the room. Morula had long forbidden access to her room, and Estelle was scandalized to behold the disorder that reigned there. Romance novels were piled everywhere on the floor, the venetian blinds had been raised on one side only, the lamp had tipped over, and the bed was in a state of total disarray. Estelle noted so many violations of the Delorme Household Rule Book that she stopped counting.

"Something smells funny in here," she said, "and I don't mean the musty odour ..."

Morula's pasty-mouthed protestations notwithstanding, Estelle's practised nose caught a scent buried deep in her memory, one that had left an indelible trace. The odour she captured was that of vanilla, she was sure, and she quickly located its point of origin: the armoire. One by one she pulled open the drawers to the clatter of empty vials. There must have been three hundred in there!

"Judging from the eighty-nine-cent price stickers on these bottles," Estelle calculated aloud, "the amount you have squandered represents no less than two hundred and sixty-seven dollars. Don't try to convince me you paid that out of your pocket money ..."

The sum was so immense that Morula herself was speechless. She quickly confessed, displaying her vanilla-blackened teeth.

"I put aside the money by cutting back on dry-goods expenses."

What would be the punishment for a crime of such gravity? A simple fine would not be enough to guarantee against repeat episodes. Exemplary punishment was called for.

"I hereby sentence you to solitary confinement," Estelle declared. "You will not leave your room until the end of summer."

"But Penny invited me to the opening of the shopping centre next week! I must absolutely attend."

Her voice was breaking with despair, but that failed to move Estelle, who left the room and locked the door behind her.

But before she did, she told her, "Let that be a lesson to you."

Then, twisting the knife in the wound, she added, "I'll send Blastula instead of you. She should truly enjoy herself."

1937

A calculated risk: that was a fitting description for Louis-Dollard's life until fate placed Estelle on his path. Since childhood, he had always demonstrated a keen sense of actuarial prudence, attempting to foresee the consequences of each of his decisions in order to maximize the prospect of gains and minimize the possibility of losses. Those same considerations shaped his ambition to one day become a prosperous landlord – real estate represented, for him, an ironclad return on investment.

He devoted much of his time to observing the construction site as the Enclave was being built, and he concluded that the promoter's profession required little talent, except for keeping the purse strings tightly drawn. At age twenty-five, when he received from his father a handsome sum to launch his own business, his strategy was already in place. All that remained was to wait for the gold-plated opportunity.

It was not long in coming. Our dear Mayor Darling, mindful of the need to increase municipal revenues in those times of crisis, committed himself to doubling the population. In twenty years of existence, the Enclave had been able to attract only eighteen hundred residents, who lived in brand-new attached cottages and model homes with garages, yards, and porches – a small number, given the advantages the suburb offered: two schools, three churches, a multitude of nearby shops, and a bank. The mayor drew up plans for a project that included the construction of a good dozen apartment buildings in the very centre of the municipality, surrounding a large bell-shaped park baptized Connaught Park in honour of His Royal Highness Prince Arthur, Duke of Connaught and Strathearn, the third son and favourite of Queen Victoria, and who held the position of Governor General when our glorious suburb was founded.

On the day the lots were to be auctioned off to the highest bidder, Louis-Dollard was among those best positioned to profit. He set his sights on a lot that enjoyed an exceptional location next to the bank, and purchased it at a fire-sale price.

"There will be certain restrictions," the mayor warned. "The city reserves the right to approve the plans, and construction costs must exceed five thousand dollars."

Louis-Dollard had no intention of unduly exceeding the obligatory minimum. He prepared the preliminary sketches and estimates himself, hiring an architect only to execute the final drawings. He had the good fortune to deal with a certain Émile Monet, who understood very well what Louis-Dollard was looking for. As well, the architect was able to provide him with the names of several suppliers, including his brother, who had been a locksmith.

"He died last year, but the family took over his shop," he explained to Louis-Dollard. "If you tell Estelle I sent you, she will give you a substantial reduction on the price of materials."

"Is she the widow?"

"No, the eldest daughter. But I warn you: don't try to put one over on her. She has a remarkable nose for business."

ຕຕ

The locksmith's shop was located on Ontario Street, at the corner of Morgan. As façades go, it was hardly remarkable: the show window displayed three padlocks. Inside, the space was so narrow that Louis-Dollard had no trouble finding the woman named Estelle. She did not seem ugly to him, though she was far from being a beauty. Her main quality was that she was still young, though four years his senior. She was hunched over a small workbench, busy making a key.

"How may I be of assistance to you?" she said without looking up from her work.

Louis-Dollard handed her his list, which she read in a loud voice after adjusting her glasses, punctuating the name of each article with an affirmative nod of her head.

"I have everything in stock," she said, "but I will need more than an hour to prepare the order."

"I am in no hurry," answered Louis-Dollard, already looking forward to drawing out his visit.

"I must request that you pay today, however. We do not give credit to anyone."

"Your uncle, Monet the architect, sent me," Louis-Dollard added. "I am about to begin construction of a building, and if you are prepared to offer me a good price, I will become a regular customer at your shop."

Estelle looked him in the eye.

"I can offer you a discount of 5 percent."

Louis-Dollard took a step in her direction and leaned against the counter.

"Why not ten?" he said in a low tone.

With a sigh of resignation, the young woman prepared the bill.

"It will take me a while," she continued. "In the meantime, do not speak to me and, above all, do not touch anything."

Louis-Dollard took a seat on the bench and leaned back, so as to better observe Estelle while she filled the order, opening and closing the drawers that contained the locks, the latches, the padlocks, and the bolts he had requested. She accomplished everything with great precision and even greater economy.

When she had finished and it was time to pay, Louis-Dollard could not restrain himself from expressing his admiration for her efficiency. First she counted the money reverentially, smoothing out the banknotes as if she were ironing them, and placing the coins with great care in their compartments as though they were made of glass. Once the cash drawer was closed, she took off her glasses.

"I was brought up on locks, and I know their workings by heart ..."

Louis-Dollard returned home light-footed, his heart overflowing with joy. It was only that evening, after having undressed, that he examined the receipt the young lady had prepared for him. Not only had she neglected to apply the promised discount, she had raised the prices by 10 percent!

ෆෑ

"Estelle? Really?" Monet the architect said in surprise when Louis-Dollard announced the following day that he had met his Waterloo, and wished to marry her then and there.

"Never in my life have I felt so strong a conviction."

"If I were you, I would think twice. She is hardly even-tempered, and I must warn you: her heart is not in the right place ..."

He related how, when Estelle was a little girl, she would beg her father for twenty-five cents to get a tooth pulled: fifteen cents for the operation, and ten for the laughing gas. Then she would instruct the dentist not to use gas, and keep the extra ten cents for herself.

"Consider yourself warned, Monsieur Delorme. My niece will never love you as much as she loves money."

Those words were music to Louis-Dollard's ears, and he left the architect's office more determined than ever to ask for Estelle's hand.

"Devil take prudence," he said to himself. "I am prepared to marry her at my own risk – or fortune."

The following Saturday he presented himself at the widow

Monet's house, bearing a letter of introduction signed by the architect. He asked for Estelle's hand, and before his words had settled, he promised to find someone to replace her at the locksmith's. Her mother, whose greyish complexion and extreme gauntness prefigured her imminent death, warned Louis-Dollard not to expect any dowry other than the modest trousseau her daughter had assembled.

"I shall still come out ahead," proclaimed the suitor, "for a woman with a nose for business is worth her weight in gold."

ೞ

No sooner had Estelle given her consent than the betrothal was announced and the banns published in the Hochelaga parish. The wedding, attended only by the witnesses, was celebrated in the small chapel attached to the Church of the Nativity. The bride was attired simply in her Sunday best and her communion veil. She had created her own bouquet with dandelions picked along the sidewalk.

As the newlyweds had arranged for no refreshments after the ceremony, they set off on their honeymoon without delay. At the harbour terminus, they boarded the 49 tram. Louis-Dollard had mapped out an itinerary that would allow them to travel on all the lines of the streetcar network without passing the same stop twice. The method he used to solve this puzzle rivalled the one thought up by Euler to elucidate the problem of the seven bridges of Königsberg. Estelle, who had never set foot west of Berri Street, insisted on sitting in the first row of the conveyance, where the view was better than in the back.

And so they criss-crossed the city on a single transfer, dismounting only at the Inspector Street terminus. From there, their legs carried them to a small shack in the centre of a vacant lot. Nothing suggested that this wooden structure with the sloping roof was a railway station. No signboard, no waiting room, no newsstand, no hanging clock, no left-luggage wicket, and no platform – only three staircases that descended toward as many boarding platforms serving five lines, which converged toward a tunnel indicated by a signboard on which someone had sloppily painted the words "South Portal."

At the wicket, Louis-Dollard purchased two tickets good for one trip to the Enclave station. The clerk punched them and a porter looked after the baggage. Estelle did not fancy being thrust into darkness when the train entered the south entrance to the tunnel and the dynamo-powered lights were slow to illuminate. Why pay twenty-five cents a ticket if there was nothing to see? Louis-Dollard agreed: it was a fine waste of hard-earned money, though he spent the entire trip with his nose against the glass, amazed by the subterranean gallery that had been carved out by pick and shovel through the rocky core of Mont Royal.

Estelle's first sight of the Enclave was the station platform, laid out at the bottom of a wide trench, and she was far from charmed. But she rapidly changed her mind after climbing to the top of the stairs leading to the station, when the panorama of our little town lay before her in all its picturesque glory. The truck farms among which Louis-Dollard grew up had long since vanished, but in the eyes of a young lady from Morgan Avenue, this suburb was practically the country. Her first impression was to remain with her, and all through her life she never stopped repeating with the same fervour, "The air is purer in the Enclave than anywhere else."

༄

The newlyweds were welcomed into the ancestral home by Prosper Delorme and Oscar, the youngest son. In a glance, Estelle sized up the two men. Her father-in-law was a loathsome old man, but she felt a certain sympathy for him and had little doubt he would be easy to tame. Her brother-in-law, on the other hand, displeased her instinctively. With his overly polite smile and excessively courteous manners, he was the archetype of the prodigal son who squandered his energy on frivolous activities. Clockmaking was his true passion, and he spent hours disassembling and reassembling the movement of an old watch with a shameless complacency of which Estelle could only disapprove.

Morula, Gastrula, and Blastula no longer lived at home, having recently been sent to the novitiate of the Sisters of Saint Anne to relieve the family of their presence. Their room was vacant, and it was there the young couple settled in. Louis-Dollard suggested they join two of the twin beds to form a nuptial chamber, but Estelle quickly put a stop to any such idea.

"With the construction site to supervise," she argued, "you will need every hour of sleep you can get. As for me, I will have my hands full, for I intend to make myself indispensable in this household. No one will accuse me of being just another mouth to feed."

She had no cause for concern. Prosper and Oscar, who had to get along on their own after the girls left, were only too happy to hand over the domestic reins to Estelle. Her father-in-law happily submitted to the many rules she promptly introduced. At first he seemed distant toward his daughter-in-law, but he was quickly won over by her prowess at home economy. Not only did she husband the household resources, she generated revenue! Every morning she was up before dawn, preparing a broth made from potato peels and radish tops, which she sold for five cents a bowl to the construction workers – a more than reasonable price, considering she charged twice that amount for use of the toilets in the backyard.

No doubt about it, she well deserved her initiation into the cult of Her Majesty. One fine morning, in an atmosphere of mystery, Prosper led her down into the family chapel. The cellar had changed considerably over the past twenty years.

The vegetable crates and the shelves where jam jars once stood in straight lines had been taken apart and their wood reused to build a confessional where, on the first Friday of every month, the Delormes would come to seek forgiveness for their slightest expenses. But it was the ceiling that had undergone the most striking change. Prosper had daubed the coins that lined the vault with pregnant mare's urine, and on contact, the copper had taken on a rich patina of verdigris that lent the space the feel of a long-neglected tomb. At the sight of the mosaic, where the countenance of Her Majesty appeared reflected ad infinitum, Estelle fell to her knees, enraptured.

Prosper endeavoured to evangelize his daughter-in-law on the spot but quickly realized he was preaching to the converted. Better yet: her exemplary devotion to money made her a most pious believer. And since one day she would transmit the true faith to her heirs, the patriarch did not hesitate to entrust her with a personal, indeed an intimate, secret – one he had never revealed to anyone.

৶৶

Prosper was all of eleven years old. After a long day picking apples in the orchard, he had paused to rest against the fence before returning home. The air was as crisp as the flesh of the apple he had bitten into, and the sun was declining with the dazzling intensity it possesses at the equinox. From down the road a horse-drawn carriage was approaching at high speed. It was driven by a man clad in black, dressed as city dwellers did. It was Dr. Simon, the new parish physician. He had been expected the previous day at the Deslauriers house to amputate little Charles's leg, turned gangrenous from a farm accident. But the doctor had been delayed by a childbirth and now feared he might lose his way on the country roads and arrive too late to save his patient.

He pulled to a sudden stop next to Prosper and asked

point-blank for directions. The lad was unmoved by his impatient, somewhat imperious manner, and was in no hurry to respond. A familiar feeling held him back: an instinctive and near insurmountable reticence to share that which belonged to him, even the most elementary information.

"Cat got your tongue?" snapped the doctor, becoming more agitated by the minute.

There was no one else in sight, and Prosper was the only one who could help him – a situation that could be used to the boy's advantage.

"A bit of information should be worth something," he said to the physician as he gnawed the core of the apple he was eating.

Dr. Simon adjusted his spectacles and took a deep breath. In normal circumstances he would have stepped down from his carriage and given the little scoundrel's ear a pull. But since every second counted, he tossed him the only coin he could find in his vest pocket and with a snap of the whip sent his horse galloping off in the direction Prosper indicated.

The lad took care not to show his parents the product of his extortion. He waited until night fell to examine, in the secrecy of his room by the flickering light of a candle, the first coin he had earned in his life. The coin, minted in 1880, was of pure silver with a face value of twenty-five cents. The obverse bore the effigy, in profile, of Queen Victoria with her ceremonial diadem, and the reverse, a wreath of maple leaves. Never had Prosper held anything so precious, and he did not regret having used such a sordid stratagem to lay hands on it.

He would soon have more reason to congratulate himself, for the coin caused a veritable cascade of manna to descend upon him. The very next day, he received two cents from the beadle for having helped him find the collection basket, and two days later, a widow gave him five for retrieving her hat that the wind had blown off. The following Saturday, he sold the six chickens he had taken to market for an unhoped-for price, and his father let him keep a few cents of the profit. Not to mention the excess change he'd been handed at the general store, which he unscrupulously pocketed.

This sudden reversal of fortune was not fortuitous, reasoned Prosper when, come evening, he spread out his treasure on the cover of his straw mattress. He placed the silver coin in the middle, like a fecund hen surrounded by her clutch of chicks. The rest of the time, he kept it securely on his person, and rubbed it between his fingers at every opportunity, as much out of superstition as to confirm that it was still in his possession. He soon came to look upon it as a talisman and never, over the ensuing half-century, was he to part with it even though, on subsequently minted coins, three sovereigns had succeeded one another.

ოუ

In the manner of a pendulum as Estelle looked on, Prosper dangled the venerable coin, which was so time worn that the wreath of maple leaves could barely be distinguished, and even less so the Queen's features.

"This is the Mother Coin," he said solemnly, "the origin of our fortune. She generates wealth, and he who possesses her will never want for money. At my death, it will devolve to the first of my heirs."

That very evening, Estelle raised the subject of his conjugal duty with Louis-Dollard, and submitted to him in the fevered hope of conceiving a child – preferably a son. The matter was rapidly consummated: to ensure optimal output with minimal investment in energy, Estelle counted the movements while Louis-Dollard performed like a revolver, with six short thrusts delivered in quick succession. That method of copulation must have been dreadfully effective, for the young couple was soon able to announce to Prosper that the continuation of his bloodline was assured.

Estelle made the most of her condition to limit her activities and lounge in bed. Come summer, she would spend afternoons reclining on the front porch, claiming the heat indisposed her. Around four o'clock, when the ice-cream vendor's bell rang, she would feel a sudden craving and rush down to the three-wheeled ice-cream cart and, for five cents, purchase a Neapolitan cone – vanilla, strawberry, and chocolate. She would lick it languidly as she rocked back and forth, and when the scoop began to soften, she would push it down into the cone with her tongue. Then, head back, she'd bite off the tip of the cone and suck the melting ice cream through the hole. But since she felt guilty about spending her hard-earned pennies, she had calculated how much this small pleasure would cost her over the year. The sum of eighteen dollars and twenty-five cents all but nauseated her. She needed only a slight extrapolation to conclude that before her death she would enrich itinerant vendors to the tune of one thousand dollars! Then and there she foreswore ice-cream cones. Henceforth, she would suck on coins instead.

And so, with her conscience at peace and her spirits serene, she gave birth to a son, to the great joy of her father-in-law. She set up a cradle for the newborn in one of the drawers of the dresser and cut diapers from newsprint, which she fastened with clothespins. She breastfed him, and forced the milk he regurgitated back down his throat to teach him the horror of waste, despite his young age. She herself drank strongly hopped porter to stimulate her mammary glands, hoping that way to extend the period of lactation to at least four years, and so delay the time when she would have to purchase Pablum, the new miracle cereal everyone was feeding their babies.

At three months the infant had not yet been given a name, and Prosper insisted he be baptized. One fine Sunday, while all the Enclave's good Christian folk were at church, the patriarch sought out the young parents and informed them that the ritual would soon begin. The child had been ready since dawn, Estelle replied, and together they made their way down to the cellar, where Oscar awaited them. The chapel door was wide open and a tallow candle had been lit.

Prosper had donned his black suit and shiny black boots for the occasion. He took the nursling from Estelle's arms and rubbed the tip of each of his fingers with the Mother Coin as he intoned as in an incantation.

"By the power of His Majesty, King George VI, I baptize you Vincent. May all that you touch henceforth be multiplied by twentyfold and one hundredfold."

He was about to proceed with the benediction, but he was interrupted by the sound of women's voices coming from the front porch, followed by the slamming of the door and the noise of determined footsteps. He raised his head just in time to see Morula, Gastrula, and Blastula burst into the chapel. With their rain-soaked cloaks and their bags of tricks cut from pigskin, they looked like the three witches of *Macbeth* wandering in galoshes across the moors of Forres.

"We've been expelled from the convent!" proclaimed Morula, not without a touch of pride.

"Dismissed! Excommunicated!" added Gastrula. "Just because we refused to take the vows of poverty and renounce His Majesty's works and pomp."

"Why, the mother superior even called us heretics," exclaimed Blastula. "We narrowly escaped exorcism!"

The three women stepped forward and, somewhat cavalierly, introduced themselves to Estelle.

"And is this the heir to the Delorme fortune?" asked Morula, leaning over Vincent.

"The one and only," answered Estelle, in a tone that clearly signified there would be none other.

"We would not like the family fortune to be diluted in the future," added Louis-Dollard by way of explanation.

"His eyes will be as green as dollar bills," predicted Blastula.

"He will become the head of our empire," acknowledged Gastrula.

"He will become a millionaire," echoed Morula.

At that very moment, a copper coin came unstuck from the ceiling and fell upon the forehead of the newborn, who broke into shrieks of protest. Estelle interpreted his cries differently.

"He already disapproves of waste!" she said. "What a happy augury!"

ၰ

The family council convened to decide what was to be done with the three sisters, whose unexpected return had thrown the household into disorder. Estelle proposed to take them under her supervision and oversee their work. Her plan had been well thought out.

"Blastula will look after the housekeeping; Morula, the laundry and the mending; and Gastrula, the shopping and cooking."

"Very good," said Prosper. "But where will we put them?"

It was then that Oscar stepped forward.

"They can have my room," he informed his father, "as I will be leaving. It is time for me to strike out on my own. Give me a small amount of money to get established. I ask for no more than Louis-Dollard received."

"So be it," said Prosper. "Go forth, and fructify your talents."

The next day, Prosper bid his youngest son farewell. It was the last time the two would see each other, dead or alive.

1963

Each morning our street swarms with hordes of young newspaper boys, some on bicycles, others pulling little wagons, tossing onto the front porch of every house a copy of the *Star*, *La Patrie*, or the *Gazette*. But they pass me by without stopping: why would the Delormes spend ten cents for news that would be old the next day? When Louis-Dollard wanted to know the racing results, he would rise at dawn and creep on tiptoe through the corridors of the apartment building, where he would leaf through his tenants' papers. One morning, Penny Sterling caught him red-handed in front of her door, his nose buried in the sports section of *La Presse*.

"Your newspaper was delivered to our door by mistake," he said to save face. "I've come to give it to you."

"You are too kind," said Penny as she took possession of the crumpled sheets. "I can give you the sports pages if you like. I never look at them. And take the *Weekly Post* while you're at it; I've finished with it."

All the residents of the Enclave read the *Weekly Post*. That is how they keep abreast of our good mayor's latest projects, new municipal regulations, house break-ins, activities at the community centre, and the library's latest acquisitions. It is abundantly illustrated with photographs depicting weddings, the victories of our sports teams, the arrival of the duchess of the carnival at the arena, the summer parade in Connaught Park, and the armistice ceremony at the cenotaph. In its pages you can also find a list of homes that our real-estate agents have placed on the market, as well as numerous advertisements.

That day, a full-page ad announced the opening of the new shopping centre that had been built just behind the clubhouse of our late lamented golf course. From my roof I watched with fascination as the construction progressed. I looked on as workers felled venerable willow trees, dug deep trenches, poured the foundations from which walls soon emerged, finished with ultramarine-glazed bricks, and, finally, hung the signs of the thirty-seven businesses that set up shop there. Clothing and intimate apparel and shoe stores, dry-goods stores, hairdressers, restaurants, bakeries, sweet shops, florists, tobacconists, hardware stores, bookshops, pharmacies, banks, shops specializing in toys, music, and sportswear, a health club ... The newspaper provided a detailed list, including the day's schedule of activities.

When Louis-Dollard returned home, he headed straight for the dining room and eagerly showed the full-page ad to his wife, who had lingered at the breakfast table to pick up the toast crumbs with a pair of sugar tongs. Meticulously, she collected the crumbs in a metal pot so, when a sufficient quantity had been amassed, they could be used to make breadcrumbs or bread pudding.

"The shopping centre is opening. Is my sister ready? Miss Sterling promised to meet her at noon sharp in front of the fountain."

"I sent her off to change her clothes," Estelle replied. "Don't forget to give her some money, in case they go to a restaurant."

"Just between us, do you think Blastula will be a good spy?"

Without letting go of the tongs, Estelle reassured him.

"One thing is certain, she could not be worse than Morula."

On that matter, I could easily contradict her.

☙☙

Hideous black creatures. Shiny and fuzzy, trapped in obscene contortions. That was what the filth looked like beneath the lens of Blastula's microscope this morning as she examined her fingernail trimmings magnified four hundred times – dirt she had probably accumulated a few minutes earlier while counting the pennies in her change purse. How well she knew that nothing is filthier than money, especially the coins she picked up from sidewalks, gutters, beneath park benches, and coin-return slots of public telephones, and which she procured in the hope of one day acquiring an even more powerful microscope, one that would reveal to her, in all their horror, streptococci, staphylococci, pneumococci, bacilli, treponema, spirilla, and aspergilli and other varieties of mould.

Yet after handling the pennies, she had washed her hands meticulously with Cuticura soap. This famous antiseptic produced by the Potter Drug and Chemical Company contained two medicinal ingredients, triclocarban and Prussian blue, which eliminated 99.99 percent of fungi and bacteria from the skin. But a plethora of germs had obviously escaped her efforts at sterilization, and now, along with her onychophagy, they threatened her with cankers, paronychia, thrush, and ungual psoriasis. For since childhood, Blastula suffered from a loathsome habit that she had never been able to overcome: she could not keep her hands away from her mouth. She bit her nails to the quick, gnawed at her cuticles, chewed at the skin that connected the thumb to the index finger – and she preferred to do it safely.

No one in the entire household made quite such a fuss over bodily hygiene – and no one took so little care of their physical appearance. Every day she wore the same clothing: black trousers and a cotton-jersey turtleneck she had purchased from the boys' section of a mail-order catalogue, just as she had her crepe-soled shoes. She owned neither jewellery nor scarves, nor any other accessory. She never used makeup. She kept her hair in a ponytail. Of the three sisters, for Estelle to choose her to attend the fashion show in which Penny Sterling would be participating lay beyond all comprehension, for she was incontestably the least likely and most improbable candidate for this highly feminine mission. It would have been more appropriate to enrol her in a bodybuilding course at a Vic Tanny gym.

To see her donning white gloves, you would have thought she had finally made a major concession to elegance. Nothing could be further from the truth: the gloves were intended to protect her hands just in case, on her way to the shopping centre, she spotted the coppery glint of a dropped penny. She proceeded carefully, lingering at the level crossing where, after dark, the Enclave's juvenile delinquents would gather to set off firecrackers. She rummaged through the underbrush but came across only chewing gum wrappers, crumpled Kleenex, used bandages, Popsicle sticks, and rusted bottle caps.

Suddenly, the jarring blare of a brass band brought her back to reality. The sky, cloudy earlier that morning, had now cleared, and high up into its vault soared a flight of red and blue balloons. The festivities were underway at the shopping centre, and Blastula hurried her pace.

When she reached the entrance, the parking lot was already full and rubberneckers had clustered around the revolving doors of Morgan's department store. While children in strollers cried out to be taken to Fernley's toy shop or to ride the long slide that had been set up at Browns Shoes, the men sought refuge at the tobacconist's or at DeSerres, which sold sporting goods, or stood, mesmerized, in front of the Brière Lingerie show window. A throng of elegantly clad women had gathered on a broad passageway in readiness for the fashion show that was about to begin; two very distinguished ladies had come all the way from Roxboro to attend. After testing the microphone, the mistress of ceremonies called for quiet and noted that the garments being shown today were graciously provided by Dobridge's and Lindor's, two ladies' wear boutiques. Jazzy music began to pour from the loudspeakers and in short order the first models made their entrance. They walked, setting the tips of their toes on the ground before their heels, heads held high and eyes focused on nothing. Some wore fitted airline stewardess's suits, others sundresses with boleros. Their kidskin gloves reached their elbows and the brims of their hats were so wide that they could have been umbrellas. None drew as much applause as did Penny Sterling, wearing gingham capri pants and a blouse tied beneath her bust.

"Her outfit is a bit too revealing for my taste," exclaimed one of the Roxboro ladies. "But it's just perfect for the model who's wearing it."

"She has quite the figure," her mother agreed. "And it fits her to a T."

Blastula had seen and heard enough. She chose that moment to slip away and thread her way through the crowd as far as the fountains, where some of the more superstitious spectators had come to cast coins. So many pennies had accumulated in the pools that you could hardly make out the mosaics that lined it. Blastula approached the lip of the fountain, unconcerned about being splashed by the powerful jets of water. She tried to evaluate the sum of this scandalous expenditure. Then a brilliant gleam caught her eye – the gleam not of copper, nor of nickel, but most definitely of silver! Saliva so abundant flowed into her mouth that she could barely swallow.

The bells of the two Catholic churches in the Enclave sounded noon. On the passageway, the mistress of ceremonies was announcing the end of the fashion show, and the crowd began to disperse. There was no time to lose. Blastula quickly surveyed the area, and once she was sure no one was watching her, she thrust her gloved hand into the fountain with an expression of disgust at the thought of the bacteria proliferating there. As discreetly as possible, she tried to retrieve the dime, but the glove hampered her dexterity and the coin, wriggling like a silverfish, slipped between her fingers. Blastula bent over the lip of the fountain – any farther and she would have toppled into the contaminated water. She was almost there, she was just about to reach …

A voice called out and startled her.

"Have you lost something?"

Thank God, it was not a security guard but only Miss Sterling, who excused herself for being late for their meeting time. She had changed into a flared skirt with an open-collar shirt, but she was still wearing her makeup from the fashion show. Her eyelashes were lined with mascara and her lips painted an appetizing red. Sunglasses held back her abundant chestnut hair. Mortified at having been caught with her hand in the water, Blastula removed her glove and clumsily tried to wring it out.

"Let's go for lunch," said Penny while her friend waved the glove back and forth to dry it out. "You must be starving."

Instead of sitting at the Woolworth's counter with the rest of the populace, at Penny's insistence the two went into Les Cascades, a chic restaurant whose bay windows overlooked the fountains. The place was already packed and the maître d', bowing and scraping obsequiously, led them to the last free table, just in front of a wall fresco decorated with sequins in aquatic hues. The air was heavy with the odour of Freon from the air conditioners. Blastula had never set foot in a restaurant and did not know half the items on the menu. The prices seemed exorbitant, and she was concerned that she would not have enough money to pay. Luckily, her companion chose the table d'hôte at two dollars and sixty cents, and she quickly ordered the same thing. The waitress promptly brought them a glass of clam juice accompanied by two saltines individually wrapped in cellophane, followed by a filet of breaded haddock with tartar sauce and, for dessert, a slice of coconut meringue pie.

After the meal, as Blastula sipped her tea – premium-quality Salada orange pekoe – Penny leaned toward her and spoke in a confidential tone.

"I hope you don't find my comments out of place, but your hands seem red and irritated."

"I can't help it. They soak in a bucket of Javex all day and only come out to scour the countertops with Old Dutch Cleanser."

"But that powder is extremely abrasive! It's made of pumice stone from the Mojave Desert, in California!"

"And when I finish cleaning the house, I have to scrub my hands with Cuticura to disinfect them."

"You must be suffering from dermatitis. Your problem used to be common among operating-room nurses. Their hands often became irritated by the antiseptics used during surgery."

To relieve them, Penny related, the great surgeon Halsted of Johns Hopkins Hospital in Baltimore invented rubber gloves. He had them made in the Goodyear factory, where they used sulphur to vulcanize latex. The process guaranteed a perfect barrier against any form of contamination.

"You will be happy to learn, Mademoiselle Delorme, that the Playtex company has introduced rubber gloves especially designed for housekeeping and dishwashing, and you can pick up a dime wearing them, if their advertising is to be believed."

"Where can I buy them?"

"At Woolworth's. They cost one dollar and thirty-nine cents a pair."

Blastula's eyes lit up with a covetous glow and she leaped to her feet.

"Then what are we doing here?"

She was in such a hurry she abandoned Penny to pay for the meal. As a tip, she left her water-soaked cotton glove on the tablecloth.

తని

Blastula strode out of Woolworth's fifteen minutes later wearing bright canary-yellow gloves. She was all the prouder at not having paid for them; Penny had generously given them to her as a gift. She headed straight for the fountain, eager to discover whether the rubber was truly waterproof. But her face fell when her search of the bottom yielded nothing but copper pennies. No doubt about it: a highwayman had made off with her silver coin!

And to top it off, she heard Penny exclaim behind her, "Today must be my lucky day! I just found a dime on the ground."

She turned the shiny disc over in her open palm, exposing the dimpled images whose slightest details Blastula was intimately familiar with, having often examined them under the microscope, obverse as well as reverse: first, the dignified profile of Her Majesty Queen Elizabeth II, then that of the schooner *Bluenose*, engraved by medal carver Emanuel Otto Hahn, who had also designed the caribou on twenty-five-cent pieces and the voyageurs in their canoe on the one-dollar coin.

Blastula wanted nothing better than to intercept the coin as it turned, clutch it in her grasp, and hold it close to her heart. She glared at Penny as if the young woman had stolen the money, and she felt like pulling off her gloves and biting her nails in indignation.

"You don't seem to be feeling well," said Penny.

Blastula had to admit that the day, so rich in emotions, had sent her mood swinging.

"Not to worry, Mademoiselle Delorme. I have just the thing to perk you up."

Without another word, she led her to the far end of the shopping centre, and after winking at her knowingly, pushed open the door to the candy store.

"Follow me," she said as she went in. "With this bonanza, we'll have ourselves a treat!"

Blastula knew nothing about candy outside of those disgusting cinnamon-flavoured goldfish, and she was overwhelmed by the exotic, enticing odours: cocoa butter and orange cream, maraschino cherry and Brazil nuts, nougat and sugared fruits. Behind the glass display case, a cordial saleslady suggested Penny choose a box of miniatures, "the ones ladies prefer," but Penny was not to be tempted.

"No, no! What we would like is penuche."

The saleslady used a pair of gilt tongs to grasp two squares. She wrapped each of the sweets in cellophane and placed them on the counter. Blastula felt a pang of regret when the dime – her dime! – vanished into the cash-register drawer.

As soon as they left the store, Blastula ripped open the wrapper and swallowed her square of penuche with delectation. Penny scrutinized hers from every angle. She was knowledgeable about penuche, she said: her late mother made an excellent variety. She used only 35 percent cream and genuine maple sugar. Her confections were pale yellow, sweeter than a caress, more unctuous than a dream.

"The colour of this penuche is a bit too dark," she said severely. "And it doesn't smell all that good to me. It's not the scent of natural vanilla, but a pale imitation, oil of clove."

She nibbled at the square and immediately made a face.

"Butter and plain brown sugar – what a disappointment!"

"One must always beware of imitations," Blastula intoned with a singular lack of empathy.

"I would pay handsomely to taste my mother's penuche once more," said Penny with a deep sigh of regret. "Come, let's return home."

She threw the rest of the square to the ground and walked off briskly. Before setting out after her, Blastula snapped her yellow-gloved fingers, picked up the half-eaten morsel, and slid it into her coin purse.

When she came back here, she went upstairs to her room, cleaned the square with alcohol, and buffed it until it shone like a freshly minted penny. Then she took a smear and observed it under the microscope. When she saw the penuche was perfectly sterilized, she took it to Estelle.

"Do you see this?" she said. "If you want to catch a fly, this is how you attract it."

1940

If time were truly money, as Benjamin Franklin maintained in his *Advice to a Young Tradesman*, Oscar Delorme would have been a millionaire many times over. Early on he decided to make a profit from the few elements of watchmaking he had acquired by taking apart watch movements and putting them back together, and he opened a jewellery store with the nest egg his father had given him. Unfortunately, he had not inherited the family's business sense. Instead of setting up shop on a main street, he exiled himself to the working-class district of Rosemont just as the city's economic crisis was at its deepest.

His shop, located in a building owned by the Montreal City and District Savings Bank at the corner of 7th Avenue and Masson, shared an entrance with a photo studio. Oscar spared no effort to make his shop look as luxurious as the downtown department stores: mirrors covered the walls, crystal chandeliers hung from the ceiling, purple velvet drapes embroidered with his initials framed the show windows, and solid oak display cabinets held pearl necklaces, bracelets, gold chains, and rings set with diamonds and other precious stones, as well as a wide selection of watches, clocks, eyeglass frames, and silverware of all kinds.

The budding businessman was so proud of his shop that on opening day, he had himself photographed in front of his show window, which was inscribed with silver-plated script: "Oscar Delorme, Jeweller & Watchmaker." But he had to be patient, for his neighbour was busy shooting the portrait of a young lady – and the seance promised to be a lengthy one. The subject had insisted on two different photographs. The first was destined for a suitor who preferred her hair pulled up into a bun, and the second, to another young gentleman who liked it in braids. In front of a backdrop representing a park, she posed seated on a wicker bench that she shared with a stuffed squirrel. Oscar found her pretty as a picture, and couldn't help but smile when she pretended to scold the creature. The young lady batted her eyes in his direction, and every time she smiled, he felt a powerful surge of emotion. After fifteen minutes of this routine, in exasperation the photographer suggested they pose together, which they agreed to without a moment's hesitation. They sat motionless in front of the lens, looking into each other's eyes, fingers entwined, long after the birdie had flown.

Giselle was far from being as good a catch as Estelle. She came from a modest background. Her father was a travelling salesman who had squandered the family's savings on a woman of easy virtue he kept in the lower districts. Giselle had had to leave school young to earn her living, working first in a rag-doll factory, then at a hatter's, where she began as a dresser before becoming a milliner. She had little taste for domestic tasks, and possessed a single talent: she knew how to make penuche. Once a week she went to the Marché du Nord to purchase double cream – a rare item that dairy farmers set aside for their best customers, and which could be pried out of them only with powerful supplication. Returning home, she would pour a pint into a saucepan with four cups of grated maple sugar and a teaspoon of baking soda, then boil the mixture until it formed large, solid bubbles when blown through a slotted spoon. She added a drop of vanilla extract, a knob of butter, a pinch of salt, and beat the mixture vigorously with a wooden spoon – no more than forty times, according to the secret recipe that had been handed down from mother to daughter for four generations.

Of all confections, penuche demands the greatest precision. One second too little of cooking will make crystallization impossible, and one second too many will result in a granular mass, which is why, over the years, the original recipe, scribbled on a sheet of lined paper, was adjusted, improved, and abundantly annotated until it had become a complex and studied plan that would lead to perfection every time. Only when the penuche had reached its ideal consistency could it be spread on a tray and cut into squares that would be set out for serving in an opaline fruit bowl.

This was what Giselle plied Oscar with during the two months of their courtship. In the course of their heart-to-heart conversations, he avoided speaking in too much detail of his family and the strange practices they engaged in, mentioning only in passing that they venerated nothing more than money. And to prove he was unlike the rest of his clan, he chose for his fiancée, as a token of love and gratitude, the most beautiful diamond ring in his collection – a thirty-point brilliant framed by two baguettes in a white-gold filigree cathedral setting – and wed her with neither dowry nor trousseau.

The newlyweds set up house in the apartment directly above the jewellery store. Their perfect bliss rapidly faded, as the business did not prosper. With the economic crisis, the district's factories reduced production and most of the workers were laid off. Families that had only enough to feed themselves were in no position to give watches as birthday gifts, let alone gold crosses for first communions. Oscar hit upon the idea of offering free eye tests to attract customers, who did come into the shop in greater numbers. But they entered because they had nothing else to do, and when they left empty handed, the cash register was empty too.

One day, a well-dressed gentleman with a haughty manner entered the shop. It was Louis-Dollard who, on Estelle's orders, had come to do a little snooping. At the sight of so much gold and silver so ostentatiously displayed, he was certain his brother had lost his marbles, and it came as no surprise when the younger Delorme admitted that business was going from bad to worse. Not only that, but Oscar would soon have a new mouth to feed, as Giselle was expecting a child before the new year.

"Let me help you," said Louis-Dollard, magnanimously pulling out his wallet. "How much are you asking for that pendulum clock under the glass dome?"

His eyes had come to rest on the clock face where, inscribed in gold letters, was the motto Time Is Money.

"Forty dollars," answered his brother.

"Why is it so expensive?"

"It's an anniversary clock. You wind it once a year."

"Really? What an extraordinary saving in time and energy! If you give me a family discount price – let's say ten dollars – I'll take it."

Giselle found the bargaining offensive, a despicable way of taking advantage of their difficulties. Before Oscar could surrender to temptation, she pulled him into the backroom.

"That clock was made in the Black Forest!" she pointed out. "It is out of the question to sell it for less than its true value."

But her husband argued that they urgently needed money, and it would be foolish to turn up their noses on ten dollars cash.

For the first time, Oscar and Giselle found themselves in disagreement, and it was only after a lengthy discussion that they finally settled on a 50 percent reduction. When they returned to the front of the shop to announce their decision, Louis-Dollard had departed – taking the clock with him. In its place, on the counter, they found a meagre five-dollar bill.

This shameless theft not only drove the last nail into the coffin of an honest business career, but also consummated a family betrayal from which Oscar would never recover.

Come winter the creditors, who had so far been patient, became increasingly nervous and began to claim their due through harassment, threats, and intimidation. To reimburse them, Oscar had no other choice than to close his shop and deposit his merchandise with a Jewish pawnbroker on Saint Lawrence Boulevard. He stepped out of the dusty establishment with his pockets full of money, but in such a dejected state he let the wintry blasts guide his steps, finally ending up in Chinatown without realizing how he got there.

Chilled to the bone, he stepped into one of those smoky restaurants where the customers gathered around large round tables to gnaw on chicken feet and spit out the bones onto the sawdust-covered floor. He was the only white person in the place and was observed with keen attention. The waiter spoke only Chinese, so Oscar pointed to several dishes listed on the menu, and received a bowl of noodle soup that he mistook for birds' nests, fine strips of indeterminate meat swimming in a black sauce, steamed rice, and glossy green vegetables he tried to spear with the ivory chopsticks that served as utensils. As he sipped his tea, he realized he was out of cigarettes. Calling the waiter, he mimicked a smoker's gestures. The man gave him a knowing look and pointed discreetly to an opening at the rear of the dining room.

Oscar was no innocent. He knew what was hidden behind that beaded curtain. Why, on that day, did he not disabuse the waiter but instead made his way with determination toward the narrow staircase that led to the basement? Why did he lower himself to the level of those addicts, men and women alike, who took leave of their conscience at the threshold of the opium den and cast themselves into oblivion for several hours? To numb the pains of despair, certainly. But also to anaesthetize the sting of failure that, with his father's voice, degraded him mercilessly when he compared himself to his elder brother; even the impregnable bastion of married love offered no protection from that sting.

Feeling his way through the dark basement, he dropped onto the first mattress he came to and entrusted himself entirely to the old Chinese woman who prepared the pipes as she hummed some incomprehensible words. It would not have taken much for him to lay his head against her bosom, more withered than the blue silk jacket she wore. But he settled for fastening his lips around the stem of the heavy pipe, taking care to hold the bowl above the lamp, and inhaling the wisps of still-burning smoke in short breaths. He slipped easily into the enveloping softness of opium, and it was that sensation of abandonment, more than the dazzling of the senses, that he sought to recover as soon as its effect began to wane.

ಬಇ

There was only one way for Oscar to provide for his family's subsistence: return to the Enclave and expiate his bankruptcy by placing the sweat of his brow at his brother's beck and call. He postponed the inevitable as long as he could, waiting to be reduced to the utmost extremity before facing the ultimate humiliation. He now stayed away from home for days on end, and when he returned in the evening, he was lethargic and absent. At mealtime he barely touched his food, and his sallow face was sorry to behold. He never said where he had been, and when his wife pressed the question, he answered that he had gone wandering.

Everything suggested he had been dipping into the household money, for the rainy-day fund, kept in a black varnished metal coin box decorated with red and gold motifs, was diminishing at a faster rate than Giselle was spending. She had always had unshakable trust in her husband, but now she began to rifle through his pockets, and her suspicions awakened. Though she found no money, she did come upon a rigid oblong case, too narrow to hold eyeglasses. In it, lying upon a bed of emerald velvet, lay a graduated hypodermic syringe.

Giselle was too astonished by her discovery to confront her husband, and she could not sleep that night. The next morning her worry reached new heights when two Orientals came knocking at the door. They wore hats whose brims were too broad, frock coats that were too long, and trousers that were too baggy, with chains from their gold watches that hung down to their knees. On their faces she saw the false smiles of those who carry a concealed dagger. Instinctively, Giselle folded her arms over her swelling belly and gave the Chinamen to understand, with a toss of the head, that her husband was absent. They handed her a small pouch sealed tightly with a knotted cord and asked her, in their approximate version of English, to give it to Oscar.

As Giselle closed the door, fear crept stealthily into the deepest chambers of her heart where, up until then, she had felt secure. She shuddered at the thought that the pouch was just large enough to contain a severed finger or an ear. But when she opened it, she found only white powder.

"At least," she said to herself, "the mystery of the syringe is solved."

When he returned, Oscar began by denying he knew the Chinamen, then blurted out the truth. He had become addicted to morphine; the drug now held him in its tyrannical grip and had destroyed his health. Having recently begun to spit up large amounts of blood, he consulted a doctor who confirmed his worst fears: he was stricken with an extremely virulent strain of tuberculosis – and it was incurable.

When Giselle learned of the imminent death of the man she cherished more than anything in this world, she felt her whole life collapsing. But she mustered the strength to let nothing show so as not to further deepen his suffering. Oscar's days were numbered, and so few remained … How could she blame him for trying by all possible means to lighten his pain and forget he would soon be departing this world, leaving behind a defence-less wife and orphan? She handed him his packet of morphine.

"Go prepare your injection. There's no more need to be ashamed, or hide."

ການ

Oscar soon became too feeble to rise from his bed. He lost his appetite and could swallow no more than a few crumbs of penuche now and again. He was in such a vegetative state that he hardly reacted when Giselle, after a lengthy labour, presented their son to him. She had no one to rely on, and in despair, she wrote a long letter to her father-in-law both to announce the birth of little Philippe and to inform him of the state of Oscar's health, urging him to waste no time if he wanted to see his son one last time. She couldn't believe he would remain deaf to her call and hoped his visit would bring, if not some comfort, at least financial assistance. But the days passed, and she waited in vain.

To her disappointment, it was Estelle who showed up one fine morning, and she had to invite her in. Her sister-in-law took the trouble to remove her galoshes, but kept on her coat and the grey fur stole she herself had fashioned from the skins of mice so imprudent as to fall into her traps. Aside from the fact that it was very cold in the apartment, she was in no mood to stay any longer than necessary. She was carrying a letter from the Delorme patriarch who could not travel following an attack of apoplexy at the bank.

"They found him unconscious on the floor in the safety-deposit-box room," she related. "When he woke up, he was paralyzed on one side. They brought him home in an ambulance, and since then he hasn't gotten out of bed."

She didn't ask after Oscar as she explored the living room, touching the drapes and taking note of the deep-pile carpets.

"If you sell all this, you should easily be able to pay for the funeral," she said to Giselle. "But don't expect any assistance from the family. You may bear our name, but you'll never be anything more than a leftover for us."

She stepped toward the cradle, leaned over the sleeping infant, and reached toward his face, as if she intended to strangle him.

"So this is the new heir ... He doesn't look anything like a Delorme. He's your spitting image."

And in a tone that brooked no reply, she added, "Take the letter to your husband. Don't worry, I'll look after the child."

In more favourable circumstances, Giselle would have expelled her then and there, and slammed the door in her face. But she preferred to overlook the slight and deal with more pressing matters.

Estelle had not volunteered to visit her dying brother-in-law out of the goodness of her heart. She hoped to make off with an anniversary clock to match the one Louis-Dollard had obtained for such a good price, or maybe a piece of silver that had survived the store's bankruptcy. She turned away from the cradle as soon as Giselle disappeared into Oscar's room and began to rummage through the apartment. There was no sign of a clock, but she did come upon something almost as attractive on the kitchen table: an opaline fruit bowl filled with divine-smelling, bite-sized confections.

The five-cent pieces that Estelle sucked on every afternoon instead of a snack could not satisfy her sweet tooth. She still dreamed of ice cream, and never missed an opportunity to dip her bread in molasses or corn syrup and to chew on the beeswax from a piece of honey cake. But none of those delicacies could have prepared her for Giselle's penuche. The moment she placed a piece on her tongue, she was shaken by such a violent shock that she had to sit down. Despite herself, she began to moan with pleasure. Her sunken eyes rolled as she stuffed more penuche squares into her mouth without taking the trouble to taste them, so avidly that she soon demolished the entire bowl.

Wasn't there any more? she wondered, looking around the kitchen that Giselle had not had time to clean. The deep pot with its wooden spoon still stood atop the range. On the counter, between the empty cream bottle and the flask of vanilla extract, lay a yellowed piece of lined paper covered with convoluted hieroglyphs that reminded Estelle of some abstruse alchemical formula. The few words she was able to decipher were enough for her to understand that she held the precious penuche recipe in her hands.

She felt a bilious surge of envy at the thought of all the happiness the recipe had provided through the years, and then a flush of jealousy at the idea that anyone else but her might profit from it. With the same animosity she ripped the last page out of library books to spoil the pleasure of other readers, her first impulse was to tear up the recipe. But then she thought twice and decided it would be wiser to keep it. She folded the sheet in four, slipped it into the pocket of her mouse-fur stole, and crept noiselessly out of the apartment.

ෲ

The letter Prosper had written to his son Oscar in a trembling hand began this way:

> *No more than eight weeks remain before Victoria Day, meaning that for those who have not obeyed the commandments of Her Majesty, a mortal sin will be ascribed to their conscience. I worry for you, my poor child. I cannot believe you will end your life damned like the lost. Repent before it is too late. Have no illusions: you are gravely ill and at death's door. Pray ardently and concern yourself not with your heir: by the terms of my last will and testament, your portion will naturally fall to him.*

Despite his feeble state, Oscar was deeply touched by those comforting words.

"I have been a poor provider," he said to Giselle between death rattles, "and I die guilty of leaving you in poverty. But do not fear for the future of our son: my father will see to him. In the meantime, you may count on my family if you are in need."

Giselle was weeping with the final lamentations and did not dare contradict him. She left him to sleep in peace, knowing he would never awake again.

౨౿

Estelle informed Prosper of the death of his youngest son, going to some length to point out in no uncertain terms that not only had he died an indigent, but an atheist, an apostate, and a renegade as well. She might as well have plunged a dagger into the old man's heart. In no time, he lost all appetite for business, and even stopped his daily calculations of the interest earned on his savings account. Sensing that the end was nigh, he called Louis-Dollard to his bedside.

"I'm not long for this world," he said, "and my only regret is that I cannot take the Mother Coin with me. Watch over her as you would the goose that lays the golden eggs. Come what may, do whatever it takes to keep her in the family."

Louis-Dollard had no difficulty swearing that, but he had to pry the Mother Coin from his father's grasp. Only then did the patriarch's head slump back on the pillow, for he was sick at heart.

"Now summon your sisters and pray for me in the family chapel."

Estelle had been standing in the doorway alongside little Vincent, and did not follow the others into the basement. She slipped into her father-in-law's room and began to search for his will. Given the monastic furnishings, she had no trouble finding it stuck behind the portrait of King George VI.

The document, drawn up by a certain Robert Comtois, had been signed by Prosper on January 31, 1915, and had never been amended. Having declared himself of sound mind, body, memory, judgment, and understanding, the testator set forth his last wishes as follows:

1.   *I commend my soul to His Majesty and pray that the entries in his Great Ledger confirm my station among his chosen.*

2.   *In order that no expense be incurred for my burial, my body will be inhumed in a common grave in the paupers' cemetery.*

3.   *Never having borrowed and dying without debt, I caution my heirs against any self-styled creditor who might make a claim following my death.*

4.   *I bequeath my worldly goods, and all movable and immovable property, equally between Louis-Dollard and Oscar Delorme, my legitimate sons, in order that they preserve and fructify it.*

5.   *I desire that in the event of the death of either, his portion be given to his legitimate heirs or, should they still be minors, that it be deposited in an escrow account by their legal guardian until the attainment of the age of majority.*

It was exactly as Estelle feared: half the fortune would fall to little Philippe who, for all one knew, had inherited Oscar's disastrous business sense and would be reared by a mother who had no concept of economy. Happily, it was not too late to correct the situation, provided that she took immediate action, and preferably on her own initiative. She dipped her pen into the inkwell and, without hesitation, added at the bottom of the document the word "Codicil," which she underlined twice before continuing:

> *The present codicil revokes article 5 of my last will and testament and takes precedence over it, for it perfectly expresses my last wishes and prescriptions. As my son Oscar has died and his son, Philippe, is a minor, I declare my son Louis-Dollard to be my sole legatee to whom I bequeath all my possessions in order that he use, enjoy, and dispose of them as he sees fit.*

She went to Prosper's bedside. Taking advantage of his weakened state, she convinced him to sign the document. Too feeble to write his name, the patriarch could only scratch an *X*. All that remained was to have the codicil signed by two disinterested witnesses. Estelle did not have far to look: she hailed two passersby who, for modest compensation, authenticated the dying man's initials.

To assuage her conscience, the following day she sent Philippe a box of used clothing that Vincent had outgrown, accompanied by a letter in which she advised her sister-in-law, in the clearest possible terms, to recognize her generosity and expect nothing further from the will.

The box was sent back by return mail, with nary a word of thanks.

1963

As on the first of every month, the Delormes were in a state of high alert, for this was the blessed day when the tenants would come to pay their rent. All day until evening, my doorbell would ring like a cash register and my front door would swing open grandly upon the comforting sight of a multitude of hands humbly proffering their due. In normal circumstances, I would capture the excitement in the vestibule, behind the wicket where Louis-Dollard signed the receipts. But that morning, the epicentre of activity had been transported to the dining room, for it was there that Estelle, mouse-fur stole draped over her shoulders, was preparing her plan for the day.

Once Penny Sterling arrived, Louis-Dollard would show her into the living room and invite her to be seated in one of the leather armchairs. On the end table would be placed a porcelain tea service (that a missionary uncle had brought back from China and had never been used) and, in the centre, a hand-painted blue plate. There! The trap had been set. All that remained was to bait it.

Ever since Blastula had brought her that square of penuche, Estelle had not stopped sniffing it, even licking it, just enough to deem it of poor quality – and regret the intense pleasure she had felt, twenty-three years earlier, when she tasted Giselle's. The more closely she examined the traces of Penny's teeth, the more she was inclined to congratulate herself for thinking of preserving the stolen recipe, still tucked away in the pocket of her mouse-fur stole. Of course she would have to purchase cream and maple sugar, and those ingredients were costly. But, as luck would have it, there must have been at least seventy-five dollars in petty cash.

When she entered the office, she caught Louis-Dollard moving paper clips across the blotter, clicking his tongue in imitation of galloping horses. When she asked him for money to run errands, he replied distractedly.

"The sulkies or the steeplechase?"

Estelle stamped her foot and called him to order.

"Open the cash box right this minute."

He dropped the paper clips, produced the battered green metal tackle box, and placed it on the blotter.

"I may as well warn you that the petty cash is empty," he said before unlocking it.

"I don't understand. What happened to the seventy-five dollars?"

"Don't get upset, please. I can explain everything."

Estelle's foot tapped the floor with greater force, which inspired Louis-Dollard to make a clean breast of things.

"I borrowed the money and bet it at the racetrack. I intended to replace the amount that same day and invest the rest of my winnings in future wagers. I couldn't have foreseen that ..."

Estelle did not let him finish. She flew into one of those icy rages of hers that preceded the most violent storms.

"You squandered our seventy-five dollars on a horse?" she hissed through clenched teeth.

Louis-Dollard pushed his swivel chair back and gazed repentantly at the toes of his black boots.

"I'm not proud. In fact, I'm ashamed ..."

"You abused my trust by embezzling money from the petty cash. And you have violated the eighth commandment, which clearly states: 'Thou shalt not gamble.'"

"I have confessed my fault to Her Majesty with the sincerest possible contrition. I am prepared to swear, on a copy of *The Wealth of Nations*, never to do it again."

"You have not committed a mere mistake, Louis-Dollard – you are in a state of mortal sin. Consequently, you may no longer carry the title of head of the family. Pack your bags and leave this house immediately."

My venerable founder was stunned by the severity of the sentence.

"But, Estelle, this is my first offence. And that is in itself an extenuating circumstance ... I implore your magnanimity and your clemency."

"I am prepared to commute your sentence on one condition: that you repay me what you have stolen one hundred times over. Take it or leave it."

"Where do you want me to go in the meantime?"

"Consider yourself fortunate that I'm letting you stay in the garage. And now, out of my sight!"

The poor man had never been so humiliated in his life. As I watched him leave my premises with his belongings in a sack over his shoulder and his tail between his legs, I almost pitied him.

తఠు

After Morula and Louis-Dollard's defections, it became clear that Estelle could count on no one but herself. But the urgent situation – the imminent arrival of Penny Sterling – forced our matron to seek assistance. She requisitioned Blastula for the deposit wicket. And to Gastrula, she handed the weighty responsibility of preparing penuche.

"You need only follow the instructions to the letter," she said, handing her the stolen recipe.

Gastrula took a moment to peruse the list of ingredients.

"Cream!" she exclaimed. "I certainly have none on hand. And

there is no vanilla left in the bottles you confiscated. Morula saw to that!"

"Find substitutes for whatever you are missing. You always manage so well with what you have on hand ..."

The sweet odour that arose from the yellowed paper made Gastrula's head spin, and her eyes rolled and the sinews on her scrawny neck protruded. Our cook, it must be said, suffered from an unfortunate hypersensitivity of the olfactory nerve that made her prone to nausea. During her constitutionals, she walked briskly to avoid the pestilence of canine droppings, the deleterious emissions of exhaust pipes, and the smoke from burning tobacco. Nothing quite so offended her nose as the smell of food. Each visit to the grocery store was a trial close to torture, for the air heavy with the stench of onions, cabbage, fish, raw meat, and aged cheese summoned up images of garbage dumps or Roman orgies. At the table, she served herself child-sized portions, pecked at her food through pursed lips with a total lack of appetite, and pushed away her half-finished plate. That explained her emaciated appearance – and her loathing of the overweight for their shameless complacency and raucous joie de vivre.

In these conditions, how did she manage to prepare family meals? It was simple enough: everything she made was bland and tasteless. She refrained from using salt and cooked every-thing in water over low heat. She preferred root vegetables that grew in the dark and smelled of soil, fruits low in sugar, flavourless boiled beef, skimmed milk and white bread, soda crackers, blancmange, and rice pudding. In my pantry you did not find any of those charmingly decorated small spice jars, nor bunches of herbs hung to dry. To tickle my taste buds, I had to rely on the fragrant aroma of roasting chicken or grilled steak borne on the breeze from neighbouring houses.

Gastrula foresaw that the preparation of penuche would cause her queasiness and other disagreeable symptoms, so she threw open the windows wide before dumping a block of rock-hard brown sugar and a half-pint of milk in the pot, then stirring the contents from as far away as possible, holding the wooden spoon at the end of her outstretched arm like a witch preparing a magic brew. Over high heat, the mixture came to a rapid boil and expanded so quickly it threatened to overflow the pot. Once it had subsided, the slow process of reduction began. At the end of this crucial step, Gastrula should have added the spoonful of vanilla, but since she had no other condiment on hand, she added a dash of fusty Worcestershire sauce. Paying no heed to Giselle's handwritten instructions in the margins of the recipe, she beat the sugar mixture so vigorously it crystallized too quickly and coalesced into a hard, brittle mass. Armed with an angle iron, she tried to hack out even squares, but managed to extract only broken pieces that she heaped willy-nilly on a serving dish. Gastrula suddenly felt faint. No matter how tightly she held her nose, she could not help but absorb the sugary, volatile matter in the kitchen air now befouled by the evaporation of the penuche. To avoid fainting dead away, she hastily carried the dish to the dining room, where Estelle was waiting for her visitor with obvious excitement. Gastrula handed her the cursed recipe.

"Well," she said, wiping her hands over and over on her apron. "I did my duty, but it almost cost me my stomach. You won't catch me doing that again!"

"It doesn't matter," answered Estelle, who could hardly stop herself from dipping into the penuche on the serving dish. "With this, we're bound to ensnare our wealthy prey."

ಬಬ

So this is what a thirty-thousand-dollar fortune looks like, thought Estelle, as she looked Penny over. A creature as frail as a blade of grass.

It was true that, in her turquoise faille dress, in the midst of my austere decor, our young tenant did seem a bit ethereal. Her chestnut hair, freshly washed if one was to go by its extraordinary sheen, was gathered high on the back of her head, and it fell freely down the back of her delicate neck and the fastener of her three-strand pearl necklace. She also wore a brooch of fake coral and patent-leather pumps of matching colour. Estelle had imagined her plumper, but she was not disappointed, seeing in her sylph-like svelte nature a sign of docility, even malleability. Neck stretched like a vulture's, Estelle invited Penny to sit down beside her.

"I was just about to have a cup of tea," she said. "Would you like to join me?"

"A sip of warm water would be fine, if it's not too much to ask. To tell the truth, I can think of nothing more refreshing."

Estelle nodded in agreement.

"That is my preference as well," she said, filling the cups. "Not to mention that tea bags are truly wasteful, don't you agree?"

"Not if you use them to polish your mirrors," Penny responded spiritedly. "Afterward, you retrieve the leaves and add them to spinach purée to extend it."

Estelle had never thought of that. She was dumbfounded.

"Do you do the same thing with coffee grounds?"

"No, I use them for scouring."

"And with apple seeds?"

"Pillow stuffing."

"And banana peels?"

"I confess that, to my great disappointment, I have found only one use for them: shoe polish. Here, you can see the result!"

Estelle was powerfully impressed – and not only by the mirror shine of the coral-hued patent leather. She complimented her visitor:

"These days, young people rarely display such sense of economy."

"I was raised frugally," said Penny between sips of hot water. "I know the value of money and the importance of saving. Of course, I allow myself a few small expenditures now and then. But nothing extravagant."

"The dress you are wearing, for example?"

"It is a copy of the dress worn by Queen Elizabeth for the inauguration of the Saint Lawrence Seaway," Penny explained, blushing.

Estelle was delighted to discover in her young visitor a monarchical proclivity similar to her own.

"In my view, Her Majesty has never been lovelier than on banknotes," she said. "My son is of the same opinion."

What fable was that? Vincent loathed everything about royalty, which he considered as corrupt and degenerate as the papacy.

"Did I not hear that he is engaged and will soon be married?" inquired Penny, turning her gaze toward the clock on the mantelpiece.

"Another vicious rumour, like so many about him," Estelle protested. "Everyone is jealous of my Vincent, you understand. What young lady in the Enclave doesn't dream of snaring him? The truth is, he has not yet met the shoe that fits, if you will permit me the rather vivid expression."

"And what does this eligible bachelor do for a living?"

"He is preparing for the day when he will take over from my husband as the head of our little empire. In the meantime, he fancies himself an inventor."

Penny suppressed a yawn and inquired politely, "What has he invented?"

"Various small everyday items. When he returns from scout camp, I will ask him to show you. The two of you have a lot in common. He is also a tennis ace."

I preferred to let this grotesque exaggeration pass without comment. Silence once again fell over the room.

Noticing that Penny had put down her cup and was glancing

again at the clock, Estelle attempted to hold her back by offering her a piece of penuche from the serving dish.

"It's an old family recipe," she said, "that we reserve for grand occasions. Be my guest, taste it!"

This time, Penny's curiosity was piqued. She happily took a piece, and Estelle joined her, noting she had not eaten the delicacy for at least twenty-three years.

I could not say what first struck our guest: the granular texture of the overcooked penuche, whose sharp-edged crystals grated against her tongue, or its unidentifiable aftertaste. For a moment, I thought she would spit it out whole, but with tears in her eyes, she forced herself to swallow the whole piece. Meanwhile, Estelle shamelessly declared the thing to be "inedible."

"I am terribly disappointed," she said. "In my memory, penuche was a celestial delicacy."

"I find it quite delicious – and I know whereof I speak. Would it be impolite to ask for the recipe?"

Estelle, who felt that Giselle had deceived her, was only too happy to pull the yellow sheet of paper from her mouse-fur stole and give it to her visitor.

"It's yours!" she said sadly. "In any event, I won't be making it again any time soon."

Holding her breath, Penny accepted the offering. She unfolded the sheet of lined paper with the utmost care, since the desiccated paper was disintegrating in her hands. Her trembling fingers grazed Giselle's handwriting with the kind of veneration one normally reserves for relics. And then her eyes, moist with emotion, strayed to the mantelpiece.

"Is it already three o'clock?" she said, startled.

"Don't trust that clock. It has stopped."

"What is written on the face?"

"'Time Is Money.'"

"A wise principle, which I would do well to follow," said Penny as she rose from the sofa. "You have been so generous to me that I would not like to waste another of your precious minutes. Thank you for your kind invitation."

Estelle showed her to the door and made her promise to call again. So delighted was she by their meeting that she did not notice that Penny had departed without paying her rent.

II

SECOND FLOOR

1963

Estelle's stentorian voice finally fell silent, as had the sound of slamming doors. Time for the afternoon nap had come, and even Louis-Dollard, banished to the garage, had curled up on the back seat of the car. Lulled by the rain drumming insistently on my roof, I was just about to slip into sweet slumber when, from up the street, I caught sight of a solitary figure rushing through the downpour. My heart leaped with joy: it was Vincent hurrying home from scout camp. It was high time for him to return to the fold.

He pushed open the door and deposited his rain-soaked haversack on the floor of the vestibule. The canteen attached to it made a metallic clatter on contact with my polished tiles. He had changed so much over the course of one summer that I almost did not recognize him. His three-day beard stood out against his suntanned skin. His legs, covered with mosquito bites, were almost athletic. His adolescent awkwardness had turned to self-confidence. Most of all, there was a new sparkle in his eyes. He wore a fringed deerskin jacket and, on his head, a Davy Crockett coonskin cap. I hoped he was not intending to present himself to his mother that way: she would have an apoplectic fit.

He paused a moment to reacquaint himself with my familiar smells and, judging by his quiet self-assurance, I began to fully appreciate the inalienable ties that bound the two of us since his childhood. He surveyed the first floor and encountered no one, so made his way up the stairs three at a time. His hand, as it slid along the spine of my bannister, made me shiver faintly, and I had to admit I had missed him. I bitterly resented him last June for abandoning me to my sad fate and going off to ramble through the woods, but now that he had returned, all was forgiven. What choice did I have, in any event? He was the only hope of salvation in this household.

He strode across the landing to Estelle's room and entered with a determined step after having rapped sharply on the door. The venetian blinds had been lowered and the bedside lamp switched off, which spared me the sad spectacle of the shabby decor: the torn lampshade, the black-speckled mirror, the yellowed curtains, the faded chintz, and the lighter patch on the wall where, until a few weeks ago, the photograph of Louis-Dollard had hung. In the dim light, Vincent first made out a shapeless mass sprawled upon the bed, then the surreptitious movement of an arm making contact with a plate and hiding it beneath the pillows. He crept forward carefully and placed a kiss on his mother's exposed forehead as she began to moan.

"Can you feel how my face is burning?" she asked once she'd quickly swallowed the morsel of penuche in her mouth. "I am racked with fever. My eyelids are heavy and my limbs are pained, I cannot eat and I can't sleep at night ... How can I survive this betrayal, I ask you? I'm not long for this world, I fear."

"What happened?"

"A catastrophe: your father lost seventy-five dollars at the races!"

"Come now, that's no reason to fall into such a state!"

"Don't forget I saved that money one penny at a time. For twenty-six years I made do with dark bread and chicken necks, I collected sugar sacks to make pillowcases, I gathered discarded jack-o'-lanterns to make pie filling, I ruined my eyes darning the holes in your father's socks, and I even cut my hair to make him a toupee. I kept the purse strings tightly drawn, and what did

I ask for in return? Not even so much as a new coat! When I wanted a fur coat, I made one from the skins of mice I trapped myself. And how did he thank me? He betrayed me with a filly! I'd rather be bled dry than see the fruit of my privation end up in the dust at the racetrack. That traitor! That ingrate! Let his name never again be spoken in my presence!"

"Where is he now?"

"In quarantine, in the garage, so as not to expose us to his contagion. I also relieved him of his title as head of the family, for if we allow our fortune to fall into the hands of that inveterate gambler, it will certainly be our ruin."

"Who will administer the building now?"

"I shall keep the books and you will handle maintenance. It will be an opportunity for you to spruce yourself up, for the time has come for you to marry."

"Why such haste?"

"You're almost twenty-five, which just about makes you a confirmed bachelor."

"I feel no sense of urgency ..."

Estelle propped herself up on her pillows.

"My son, I believe you have not seized the gravity of the situation. The gangrene of prodigality has infected our family, and threatens to spread to all the apples in our barrel. Even I could well succumb. If we do not immediately adopt draconian measures, we will find ourselves on the street. There is only one way to purify our household, and that is to inject fresh blood into our line. Our prosperity is certainly worth a small sacrifice on your part."

I didn't need to see Vincent's face darken to feel his growing impatience.

"We have already discussed this matter," he said, "and my mind is made up. I have no intention of marrying Geraldine Knox."

Estelle's hand danced through the air as if dispersing dust.

"Geraldine is ancient history. That arrangement was nothing

more than an unfortunate error … a misunderstanding. In any event, that particular bridge has been burned. I have found you a candidate who possesses a personal fortune, a five-figure dowry, and an inexhaustible source of revenue, at the same time that she is a peerless housekeeper and skilled cook. She is our new tenant who, through her considerate visits, has brought me welcome comfort in my suffering."

"Is she good looking?"

"She is not hard to look at."

"If that is the case, she must not be lacking for suitors. Why should she want another?"

"I have already taken it upon myself to prepare the terrain, and she is eager to meet you. If you play your cards right, you will need to do little more than ask for her hand."

"Don't count on me to agree to one of your arranged marriages."

"For the moment, I ask only that you meet her."

"Let me empty my kit first."

Estelle backed off, but not without getting in the last word.

"Go and wash up. And do me a favour: get rid of that hat!"

ಚಲ

Vincent froze as he crossed the threshold of his room. There was a stranger seated at his desk, a slender young woman of regal bearing whom he had surprised rifling through his papers and rummaging through his drawers.

"Who are you?" he stammered. "How did you get into this house?"

Penny Sterling held out her hand and introduced herself, looking him in the eye, her cheeks displaying not the slightest touch of embarrassment.

"I didn't bother to ring," she said, "as the door was wide open."

It was I, of course, who let her in today. Yesterday as well, and on the numerous other occasions when she took advantage of nap time to slip furtively between my walls and examine my premises, room by room, with a fine-tooth comb. She worked methodically, like an archaeologist excavating a perimeter determined by a ground survey. She had almost overlooked Vincent's room, so small was it – a garret at the far end of the hallway, which doubled as a linen cupboard and broom closet. The tiny window, facing north, barely allowed the light of day to enter, and the only illumination came from a bare bulb hanging from the ceiling. Here, the parquet floor had never been varnished and the plaster walls never painted. The wadding-stuffed mattress lay atop an old metal bed frame covered by a raw wool blanket.

"What are you doing here?" asked Vincent, too confused to introduce himself.

"I came to ask after Madame Delorme and bring her a bit of penuche. She is convinced there is no finer remedy for her insomnia."

The term brought a faintly denigrating smile to Vincent's lips.

"Permit me to express a certain incredulity. My mother has never lost an hour's sleep in her life – that would be against her most deeply held principles."

"Are you her son? Madame Delorme has always praised your ingeniousness. I hope you will forgive my intrusion: I wanted to see your inventions with my own eyes!"

"You don't say," said Vincent, wrinkling his brow skeptically. "They are barely worth mentioning."

He pointed to a wall shelf upon which were aligned, alongside a piggy bank, a thermometer, a stopwatch, a measuring tape, a scale, and a series of random objects of indefinable function.

"My prototypes," he ventured, slightly embarrassed. "I made them from materials I found in the trash."

Penny slowly got to her feet, her hands behind her back. Head tilted slightly to one side, she examined the shelf as though studying a painting. She seemed perplexed, so Vincent felt moved to explain the utility of each invention.

"Do you see these two coils activated by a sardine-can opener? They form a miniature squeezing device that allows you to completely empty a tube of toothpaste with a touch of your finger. The large socket wrench you see straightens bent nails you might want to reuse, while the modified soldering iron repairs cracked candles, broken shoelaces, and even snapped rubber bands. Next to it is an old ink cartridge: it is filled with a mixture of acetone, turpentine, lemon juice, and borax that erases, quite illegally, cancellation marks from used postage stamps."

He also showed Penny a collection of Bakelite cigarette holders whose tubes were fitted with a wing nut.

"Simply insert pencil ends in them to lengthen them," he explained. "That way you can write without wasting leads and avoid a cramped phalanx."

"And the little bucket with a crank on the lid?" asked Penny, catching sight of an object abandoned to one side.

"Oh, that ... Not my greatest achievement. A centrifuge designed to extract the complete contents of canning jars and jam pots. The thing works well enough, but the process causes quite a mess. So, instead, I am trying to find a way to make the insides of the containers themselves perfectly non-stick. I estimate we could avoid wasting a million tons of food every year – more than enough to feed the hungry."

Now Penny was observing Vincent with a perplexed expression, her head tilted to one side – as though he were an impregnable strongbox.

"Did you ever consider patenting your inventions?" she asked. "You could make a pretty penny ..."

"They're just trinkets," he answered with a frown of derision, "designed to convince my mother that I am spending my free time in a healthy manner. If she knew what I was really up to, she would certainly not approve."

"You have secrets?"

"Innumerable ones, like any normal person."

"Will you tell me one if I promise not to breathe a word to Madame Delorme?"

She took a step toward him. The mischievous gleam in her eye suggested an unspoken confidence that caught Vincent by surprise. He was all the more destabilized because, for the first time in his existence, he could not quantify the emotions that surged through him: his pulse, his body temperature, his blood pressure, his breathing seemed far too rapid to be measured. Some would surely take these physiological reactions for the beginnings of some inclination, perhaps passion. I, however, knew Vincent as though I had knitted him, and I recognized the resurgence of a primordial aspiration he had abandoned, having waited in vain for it to arise. Could it possibly be that, after twenty-four years of solitude, our heir apparent had found someone in whom he could confide, someone to whom he could reveal what he had never shared with anyone?

He removed his coonskin hat, threw it onto the bed, and ran his hand through his hair. Then he confessed.

"I didn't spend summer at scout camp."

Penny's smile vanished and she held her breath.

"What did you do then?"

"I was travelling."

That little sneak, hiding things from me! I never expected such an act of insubordination. Overcome with astonishment, a few shingles came loose from my roof and were carried away on a gust of wind. Through the gaping holes, fissures, and interstices, the rain seeped into the ceiling of his room as quickly as through a sieve.

"The roof has sprung a leak," noted Penny after a drop had fallen on her head, "and right on cue: it's time for me to be on my way."

Before Vincent could react, she rose to her tiptoes and gave him a fleeting kiss, then vanished.

Vincent was still dazed when Gastrula and Blastula burst into his room like two ravens looking for a dead animal to pluck clean.

"Since when have you been inviting girls to your room?" croaked the former. "No use denying it: Penny Sterling just left, we saw her."

"This is impropriety of the worst order," piped up the latter. "You should know that, at your age."

Vincent sighed and raised his eyes toward the heavens.

"Since that is the case, I won't keep you. Go back to whatever it is you were doing – mind your own business and don't bother me."

"Just a minute, my boy," said Blastula, pulling out her magnifying glass. "You haven't passed inspection. Where are your bags?"

"I forbid you from touching them."

"Who, then, will ensure you haven't brought back some vermin from the woods?" said Gastrula. "I hope you're not counting on Morula to wash your clothes."

"I can handle that job by myself, don't you worry. By the way, where is the third Fury?"

No sooner had he asked the question than dull thudding sounds echoed from the hallway – the hammering of a fist on a door, followed by a muffled cry.

"Have pity, Vincent, deliver me!"

Vincent went toward Morula's room and saw the steel padlock that secured the door.

"There's nothing you can do for her," said Blastula, right behind him. "She has been sentenced to solitary confinement and must serve her time until summer's end."

From her dungeon, the prisoner began to cry out again.

"You'll have to soundproof the room," Gastrula informed

her nephew, "because if you don't, the neighbours will start asking questions."

"Even if you plug all the openings, it will be impossible to make it perfectly soundproof. Sound waves are transmitted not only by air, but also by vibration."

"So find some way of smothering the noise at the source – hopefully without strangling Morula. If you put your mind to it, you'll find a solution."

Vincent returned to his room and sat down at his desk. He took out his datebook and listed his chores by order of importance:

Unpack luggage.

Repair roof.

Free Morula.

Then, mustering all his courage, he wrote in capital letters at the top of the page:

See Penny Sterling again.

1942

I am all but certain that, over the span of human history, the number of children who have grown up in banks could be counted on the toes of one foot. Although, strictly speaking, I was never granted a charter, it cannot be denied that my architecture speaks of conservatism, austerity, and, above all, the inviolability of the great temples of finance. It would be hard to imagine a more inhospitable environment for a little boy – or one less propitious for his development.

And yet, for as far back as I can remember, Vincent never held it against me. He considered me his place of refuge, he felt at home within my walls, and our souls vibrated together in perfect harmony. After all, was not his constitution an extension of my skeletal structure, his arteries like my heating system, his digestive tract similar to my plumbing, his respiratory passages my windows, and his nerves, my electrical wiring? And did the two of us not bear the opprobrium of the same original sin: that of having deprived a poor orphan of his inheritance?

For the money that belonged by right to Philippe had been used to finance my construction. Of the original ancestral farm, only the family chapel was conserved. It was transformed into a strongroom, indispensable for the bank Louis-Dollard had always dreamed of. My foundations had been poured around the original cellar and the mechanism that controlled the armoured door concealed beneath the massive wood structure, which forever bound the memories that were ours to share.

Louis-Dollard made one substantial modification to the original chapel. The idea came from a certain Honoré Bienvenu, a retired lithographer, to whom he rented a comfortable five-room apartment overlooking the park. The man had worked his entire life for the British American Bank Note Company, which printed postage stamps and stock certificates, as well as the savings notes issued by the Jacques Cartier Bank, the Banque du Peuple, and the Ville-Marie Bank. He paid his first month's rent in cash, and Louis-Dollard, as was his custom, placed the bills on his blotter and brought out his magnifying glass to examine them.

"Pardon my little precautions," he said, "but I've been the unfortunate recipient of a counterfeit bill in the past."

The man countered by saying it was impossible to tell whether a bill was counterfeit by using a magnifying glass.

"Today's counterfeiters are so skilful that even an experienced lithographer would have trouble detecting irregularities in the lines of an engraving or the watermarking of the paper. Believe me, Monsieur Delorme, only the ink of a banknote cannot be imitated."

"Such ink must be indelible."

"The ink is much more than indelible! It is resistant to both acids and alkalis. Dip a banknote in vinegar and then a baking soda solution. If it is genuine, it will not be altered in the least."

Louis-Dollard pointed his magnifying glass at Bienvenu. "I remember learning in college that only gold possesses that property."

"You must have studied philosophy, then. In the sciences, you would have learned about the prodigious compounds produced by the chemical industry."

One such compound, he continued, was calcined chromium oxide. A Laval University professor, Thomas Sterry Hunt, discovered it in 1857, while working for the Geological Survey of Canada. He produced an unalterable green ink whose formula he sold to the United States Federal Reserve for next to nothing.

"The ink our federal bank uses today is an improved, patented version known as Canada Green. Calcined chromium oxide gives our banknotes their inimitable colour."

Louis-Dollard began to sniff the bills that Monsieur Bienvenu had handed him, making no attempt to conceal his greed.

"How can I thank you for sharing your trade secrets with me?" he said, making out the rent receipt. "I have always been worried that someone might counterfeit my signature, and this calcined chromium oxide ink will be very useful in protecting my documents. Do you know where I can obtain it?"

"Canada Green is not commercially available, but you can make it by mixing pigments purchased at any paint store. Simply macerate a mixture of gallnuts and gum arabic overnight, then add a pinch of heated chromium oxide to the filtered decoction. I am telling you this on a confidential basis, of course. Just imagine what would happen if the information fell into the wrong hands!"

Louis-Dollard promised Monsieur Bienvenu that he could rely on his absolute discretion, and the following day, he began to experiment using several different formulae. The ink he concocted was not quite suitable: as it dried it deposited sediment that both clogged his pen nibs and corroded them. Instead of using it for writing, he painted the walls of the paternal chapel, which was how it earned its name, the Green Chamber.

As for the Mother Coin he inherited from Prosper, Louis-Dollard embedded it in a clay brick that he fired in the furnace. It became the cornerstone upon which he would build his financial empire.

The same concern for security was evidenced in my doors, drawers, cupboards, and closets, all of which were fitted with locks by none other than Estelle.

The advantage of these sixty-seven locks was this: as Vincent was taking his first steps, I was already equipped to provide protection from the innumerable accidents that might befall an infant. Our heir could never avoid my watch and, for example, run off or defenestrate himself, or have the chance to play with matches, scald himself, or swallow quicklime. My various safety measures could not stop him from falling, but at least he never fell down the stairs. I can search from basement to attic and never recall a single moment when he was exposed to the slightest danger.

It should come as no surprise that Vincent learned to count well before he could talk. The first word Estelle taught him was "one," and the second, "two." From then on, there was no stopping him. He began by counting his eyes, his hands, his fingers, before graduating to the bars of his crib, the steps of the stairway, the tiles of the bathroom walls, the slats of the venetian blinds, and the keys on his mother's keychain. To him, cardinal numbers soon acquired the value of pronouns and functioned readily as nouns, verbs, and adverbs for describing the size, speed, and luminosity of things; their quantity was their sole quality. He was one; his parents, two; his aunts, three. His first name, a combination of the French words for twenty and one hundred, *vingt* and *cent*, rooted his very identity in the language of mathematics. Why would he need other words to apprehend the world around him or express his needs?

It was inevitable, though, that one day he would begin to speak, which happened when he reached the age of three. Before he became enmeshed in futile babbling, before he began to ask too many questions, Estelle took it upon herself to instill in him the fundamental principle of economy, the one she professed since childhood: the need to save one's saliva. She allowed him twenty words a day, and under no circumstances could he exceed that quantity.

"Words are silver, but silence is golden," she told him, by way of illustrating her point.

Once obligatory expressions, such as "if you please" and "thank you," had been deducted from the daily total, the child had little latitude to express his thoughts or participate in conversation. To avoid being cut off, he quickly learned to be concise and to use various abbreviations and shortcuts – enriching his vocabulary in remarkable fashion as he did. He soon developed a language that used gestures and facial expressions as punctuation, in which an adjective stood for a comment; an adverb, for a point of view; a conjunction, for an explanation.

He showed the same ability to adapt when his mother taught him to save his eyes in order to spare his poor parents the cost of eyeglasses later on, or when he had to present a daily itinerary of his comings and goings with a view to saving time and avoiding fatigue.

"Even though air is free," Estelle would often say, "that is no reason to waste it."

On one occasion, he braved his mother's fierce temper, and dared to exceed his quota of words by asking her, "I am bored all alone and I would like to have a friend. Why can't I play with other children?"

"Friends are a burden," she replied sharply. "They expect to be invited over for snacks, and when they invite you to their birthday parties, you have to bring them gifts."

For him the only games permitted were ones he could engage in alone: hide-and-seek played against himself, where he stood, face to the wall, counting; or treasure hunts whose goal was to enumerate the innumerable – the blades of grass on the lawn in summer, the leaves that fell from the Manitoba maple in autumn, the snowflakes fluttering through the air in winter ... When Estelle sent him out to play so as not to have to look after him, Vincent gave himself over to these activities with fervent and constantly renewed ardour, perhaps because he clung to the illusion that in his mother's heart, despite all evidence to the contrary, he still counted.

ૠૠ

On his fourth birthday, Vincent was handed over to his aunts, each of whom would in turn complete his education.

Blastula inculcated in him the fundamentals of hygiene, without which his health would be endangered.

"Think of the doctors' and dentists' fees, and the hospital and pharmacy costs you will save throughout your life if you acquire healthy habits."

After a week under her guidance, Vincent had perfectly mastered the technique of hand scrubbing with a brush and was able to apply it to the rest of his body – including behind his ears and his prepuce. He learned to cross-tuck his bed, straighten his room, and wield a broom.

Once he had learned to dress himself and fold his clothing correctly, he trained himself to play outside without getting dirty, taking care not to disturb the earth, roll in the grass, or come in contact with caterpillars and insects. Blastula would inspect him when he returned, searching for the slightest dandelion or grass stain on his trousers. After a lesson about bacteria, those tiny creatures invisible to the naked eye that infest doorknobs, he learned never to touch anything, would always sneeze into his handkerchief, and kept a respectable distance from people.

Since he didn't know the household rules yet, Gastrula had the task of teaching them to him. This was no small matter, for they numbered three hundred and sixty-five, one for each day of the year – and Vincent had to learn them by heart.

The first provisions were designed to reduce consumption of water, electricity, and heating oil. It was absolutely forbidden, for example, to bathe in more than one inch of water, leave a light on in an empty room, or "heat all of Canada" by opening the windows in the depth of winter. There followed a series of recommendations concerning the weekly allocation of cleaning and personal-hygiene products – dishwashing liquid, shoe polish, and toilet paper (a quarter-square per urination).

Gastrula watched her nephew like a hawk, never letting him put his elbows on the table (a habit that endangered the lifespan of sweaters) or drag his feet, demanding that he goose-step like Russian soldiers on Red Square. She made sure he ate every crumb on his plate, for the boy had all the appetite of a bird and was often a very picky eater. One day, when he turned up his nose on the slices of tough, grey, gristle-fibred meat that passed for roast beef at our table, she threatened him.

"If you waste food, you'll end up in the poorhouse. Finish what's on your plate. If you don't, you'll be sent to boarding school in Trois-Pistoles, where all they serve is blue potatoes."

As soon as his aunt turned her back, he slipped the pieces of meat between the dusty vanes of the cast-iron radiator behind his chair. He thought he'd gotten away with it, but Gastrula intercepted him as he was getting up from the table.

"Not so fast, young man. Pick up your meat from the floor and eat it right now, in front of me."

Of all the humiliations endured in his young life, that was among the most mortifying. Vincent was immensely relieved when, the next day, he was placed in the care of his aunt Morula.

She was charged with initiating our heir into the realities of the wider world – within, of course, the confines of the fence that encircled the Enclave. Her pedagogical program consisted of a tour of the main attractions of our fair municipality, and the tour's purpose, despite its touristic appearances, was to cultivate in the boy a healthy fear of everything foreign, in the event it might occur to him one day to venture outside my walls.

"You have to be wary," she said, beginning the lesson, "wary of everyone and everything."

She first took him to the playground at Connaught Park, where he kept his distance from the small group of happy children as his aunt explained in great detail the risks of amputation, strangulation, paralysis, and head trauma associated with the use of swings, slides, seesaws, and monkey bars. Morula also mentioned the filth in the sandboxes, since all the neighbourhood cats most surely adopted them as their toilets, and the insalubrities of the public drinking fountain, a veritable hotbed of poliomyelitis germs.

"I won't even speak of the dangers of all these big elm trees," she declared sententiously. "In the slightest breeze, a branch can fall on your head, and in a thunderstorm, the lightning can electrocute you."

Since the boy seemed unmoved by her threats, she pulled him by the sleeve to the railway station, where she warned him against the midnight train, which carried away passengers unfortunate enough to board it to the Far North, with no hope of return, and against the wild man who had taken up residence in the tunnel and lived off the tender flesh of children. On their way to the fire station, she described the giant rats that lived in the sewers and that would bite his foot right off if he splashed in one of the puddles in the gutter. At city hall she told him about the Unknown Soldier buried beneath the cenotaph, who would groan, "My golden leg!" when a person drew too close.

"It's not true!" said Vincent, his ear glued to the stone monument.

In despair, Morula led him to the far reaches of the Enclave to show him an old abandoned house, which some people claimed was haunted. Vincent stared at the hovel, a perplexed and slightly vexed look on his face.

"How can a house be hunted? I don't understand!"

Morula was discouraged. She led him back under my roof, pulling him by the arm, and informed Estelle that nothing could be done with him.

"In any case," Louis-Dollard commented, "the time has come for my son to get out from under your skirts."

And he issued a decree: from that day on, he would supervise the lad's apprenticeship.

ᖉᖈ

Louis-Dollard was shocked to discover that at age five Vincent could still not "read Arabic," so he set out to teach him to write Arabic numerals. He ushered him into his study and turned on the desk lamp, whose weak light kept the room in oppressive obscurity. He sat him down on a stool in front of a ledger, handed him a 6H pencil (the hardest, most use-resistant lead), and assigned him the task of copying out the rental register.

In the midst of this tedious exercise, Vincent made a fascinating discovery. Like the human face, numbers had physical characteristics, and it was possible to read a wide range of expressions in them: surprise, fear, anger, doubt, disgust, meanness, sadness ... Their features, straight or rounded, had the same function as the human face, suggesting wrinkled brows, wide eyes, or smiling lips. Wondering whether or not the same applied to the letters of the alphabet, he carried out a similar experiment, but after three hours, he still felt no particular emotion. And so it was confirmed: numbers, which did not have to be combined to create a particular meaning, possessed individuality like that of human beings. Lacking friends, he made them his confidants.

What would such a child possibly have done with toys? What conceivable pleasure could he have derived from acts as futile as pushing little cars across a carpet, throwing a ball, or assembling the pieces of a Meccano set? Even a tricycle or a wagon would have bored him deeply. To encourage the boy's efforts, Louis-Dollard gave him an old measuring tape. That day, a new world opened up to Vincent, a world in which things had length, width, and depth, all quantifiable variables that could be added to their numeral essence. For months he took the exact measurements of my rooms and furnishings down to a sixteenth of an inch, and entered them in his ledger. He could also observe the growth of his body and determine that the distance from his elbow to his wrist was equal to the length of his foot, and that the growth rate of his fingernails was proportional to the length of his fingers and toes.

At age six, he understood his environment according to his measuring tape. He was ready for the next stage of development, and on his birthday he received from his father a thermometer. It gave him access to a dimension whose variations were recorded by the expansion of a few globules of mercury. Did all matter contract in like manner when the air grew cooler? Did his brain increase in volume when he had a fever? He began to calculate mean temperatures and illustrate his charts with bar, pie, and line graphs. To complete his observations, he built a beam balance using a coat hanger and the lids from two jars, and he soon came to the realization that the weight of things had little relation to their volume. He developed the habit of weighing everything Gastrula bought and successfully demonstrated that the grocer had more than once attempted to cheat her. The conclusive results of his investigation won him the loftiest of recompenses: the watch whose movement his Uncle Oscar had once repaired. There were no words to describe the satisfaction Vincent derived from the timepiece. I shall simply say that, thanks to this precision instrument, he could at last indicate, in his accountant's ledger, the weekly train schedule as well as weekend and holiday arrivals and departures.

But Estelle saw these activities as nothing more than child's play. On the day Vincent turned seven, she declared that recess was over.

"You have now reached the age of reason," she said. "The time has come to send you to school and prepare you for confirmation."

She gathered up the tape measure, thermometer, scale, and watch, and placed them in front of her son. He was allowed to retain possession of only one.

"The others will now be kept under lock and key in the cupboard," she told him. "Make sure to choose wisely."

Vincent did not hesitate. He opted for the watch. When the faraway moment came when he would leave the family home, he did not want to be late.

1963

Vincent began his renovations at dawn, while I was still half-asleep. He set up his ladder in the middle of the flower beds, climbed up to the roof with a hammer, and started pounding away relentlessly. At first his blows were just another of the irritations that plague urban existence, but as the hours passed, they became like the implacable drops of Chinese water torture, and their reverberations vibrating through my rafters with growing strength caused me anticipation and fear. Now I know what anvils must feel – and I have the strongest sympathy for them.

I should not complain about all the delicate attention, but I have no obligation to be excessively grateful. When all was said and done, my new shingles were no more than plasters applied to a body that already bore multiple wounds – the proverbial finger in the dike that constantly threatened to breach. The ruination of my ruins: behold what had befallen me as a result of gross negligence. While every spring flocks of workers were busy breathing new life into my neighbours, I waited in vain for the arrival of a plumber or an electrician. For the past twenty-five years, my faded walls have not felt even the shadow of a paintbrush. I will never reach the ripe old age of the pyramids, which, being advantageously erected in the middle of the desert, do not see their foundations take on water like a leaky old boat. One day, no doubt, I will collapse like the House of Usher, and in my rubble will be buried my sinister residents and their mountain of money that could have saved me.

Vincent was not the only one up and about at that early hour. Estelle was pacing back and forth in her room, declaiming at the top of her voice a litany of complaints and reproaches against Louis-Dollard, with sweeping gestures befitting a tragedian whose dramatic effect she calculated when she passed in front of the mirror. In the kitchen, Gastrula was struggling against the nausea she experienced every morning as she prepared breakfast, with its smells of burnt toast and the obscene gasping of a woman in heat emitted by the percolator. Blastula was out picking up greasy waste paper from the front yard, dressed in her spotless white lab coat and precious yellow rubber gloves. And, lo and behold, here came Penny, carrying a box wrapped in a kraft paper bag under her arm. Just as I was about to let her inside, she was intercepted by Louis-Dollard, who had been waiting for her impatiently, lurking behind a bush, and who approached her like a whipped dog.

After twenty nights spent on the back seat of the car, my revered founder was a shadow of his former self. His hair was unkempt and his trousers appeared to have been cut from accordion pleat. Banished from the kitchen and the dining room, he had been reduced to taking his meals at the counter at Chez Deguire, a seedy snack bar. There, perched perilously atop a rotating stool and surrounded by a horde of ill-disciplined adolescents who insisted on playing the jukebox at full volume, he hastily scarfed down a sardine sandwich and a slice of Neapolitan ice cream, then fled without even a cup of coffee. He missed his wife's noodle soup and the cups of Postum she allowed him. He even missed her kicking him under the sheets. Most of all, he missed the comfort of his worn mattress.

"If I'd only known the trouble I caused you," Penny said, "I would never have passed on my friend's tips."

"Oh, I'm not blaming you – quite the contrary. I'll never

forget the excitement I felt when I stepped into the hippo-
drome, heard the starter call out, and saw the horses cross the
finish line ... I was completely in a lather. But now I am cured.
I hope you will be able to intercede with Estelle on my behalf
and convince her of my true contrition. I've written her a love
note, and would very much like to have your opinion on it."

He handed her a scrap of wrinkled paper on which Penny
could read the pathetic result of three hours of effort:

My dearest beloved, my charming and tender spouse,

*Allow me to express the fullest extent of my admiration
and esteem for your comely and intelligent person, and
the amicable sentiments I feel for you. I assure you that I
shall continue and even augment my attentiveness to you
and do all I possibly can to make you happy. That will
not be difficult, as you possess so many lovable qualities:
beauty, kindness, and pleasant temperament. I wish you
the most perfect happiness and excellent health.*

*From your husband who cherishes and adores you one
hundredfold,*

Louis-Dollard

Penny shook her head and returned the note to him.

"Fine words are worth nothing, even if they are increased
one hundredfold. Don't fool yourself, you won't get off so easily.
Your wife's forgiveness, like all things, has its price, which she
has calculated at seven thousand five hundred dollars, in case
you have forgotten."

"But it's an exorbitant sum ..."

"Is it so far beyond your means?"

Louis-Dollard hemmed and hawed, then answered, "To tell

the truth, I am far from impoverished. Unbeknownst to my wife, I set aside a private reserve in a foolproof hiding place. Do you think she would accept a personal cheque, or will she insist on cash?"

"Madame Delorme's preference for banknotes is well known, but she might also get the impression she is being bribed. I am certain that she would appreciate a small gift as a token of reconciliation. A fur coat, for example ..."

"Estelle already has a lovely stole. And besides, her change of life has given her hot flashes. What could she possibly need a coat for?"

"Don't keep trying to slip out of this. You'll only make your case worse, and damage your cause. If you want to make it back into your bedroom, you must pay, one way or another. Consider yourself fortunate. Since it's off-season, you might find one at a reduced price."

ನುಬ

"Did you bring the vanilla?" whispered Morula when she saw Penny's smiling face through the half-open door.

After Louis-Dollard left, our young tenant contrived to slip across my parquet floors without making the floorboards creak and, in the wink of an eye, she picked the lock that had kept Morula confined to her room.

"Give me your glass," she said. "I have something better."

From the kraft paper bag she pulled a long-necked bottle whose bottom was so deeply moulded that in it, as in a glass bell, was set a figurine representing a ballerina in white tutu and golden slippers. The bottle was filled with a pale-yellow liqueur in which gold spangles floated. The label read, "Lucas Bols Gold Liqueur, Produce of Holland, 60 proof, alcohol 30%." The base on which the figurine rested held a music box, and when Penny turned the key, the ballerina began to dance to the tune of Émile Waldteufel's *The Skaters' Waltz,* while the gold spangles suspended in the liqueur whirled and fluttered around her.

At the sight of the enchanting spectacle, from deep in Morula's throat issued sounds I could only describe as cooing. Its passing modulations suddenly gained speed, growing louder and faster at a dizzying rate. Never had the poor woman been possessed by such wonder. When the music box stopped and the ballerina came to a halt, she was breathless, voiceless. She held out her glass to Penny, who poured her a hearty shot of liqueur. I could smell the powerful odour of alcohol, with hints of Bourbon vanilla. Morula wet her lips and began to gurgle with contentment.

"No, no!" said Penny. "It's schnapps. You must swallow it all at once."

She obeyed with all the docility of a patient, exposing her bosom as she threw her head back.

"It's burning me!" she said, tapping her chest. "But I've never tasted anything quite so delicious."

"A little more?"

"Yes, but only a drop. Or two."

"Why don't you keep the bottle? I have another set aside."

"You are too kind, dear Penny. When I am released from here, I will recite a novena for you in our family chapel."

"The Delormes have a chapel?"

"They do indeed, right here, in the cellar. My father did the decoration. A green chamber, with a ceiling lined with coins."

"I would love to visit it …"

"Unfortunately, outsiders are not admitted."

"Couldn't you make an exception in my case?"

"Even I cannot enter it alone."

"Why such precaution for a simple chapel?"

Emboldened by the schnapps, Morula's tongue loosened.

"When my father died, the chapel's function changed slightly.

Now it is used as a vault. Don't tell a soul, but that's where our fortune is kept."

Penny bit her tongue hard to keep from reacting to the extraordinary revelation.

"You are not afraid of thieves?"

"No danger. The door is armour plated."

"But a lock is easily picked."

"The door has no lock. It is protected by a foolproof system, and only Estelle and Louis-Dollard know the combination."

"And you? You are not privy to the secret of the gods?"

"Blastula, Gastrula, and I are the poor relations in this family. My accursed sister-in-law will never let us forget it ..."

Above, on my roof, the hammer blows became less frequent, and then ceased altogether. Morula began to nod her head, on the verge of sleep. Taking advantage of her drowsiness, Penny crept away on tiptoe. Noontime was nigh, and she had other fish to fry.

ନ୍ଧ

She walked up to the foot of the ladder just as the angelus was ringing out from the church steeple. Vincent was high above her and reluctant to come down.

"Do you have fear of heights?" she asked him.

"Not at all. There's a cat lurking in the flower bed. I've tried to scare him away but he won't move."

"That big reddish cat?"

"Could you please shoo him away nicely? I don't want to hurt him by dropping my hammer."

Penny clapped her hands twice to chase away the tomcat, which took off like a shot and hid on the other side of the street.

"You must not think I'm very courageous," said Vincent when his feet touched solid ground.

"Fear of animals is normal. There's no reason to be ashamed."

"Mine was beaten into me when I was very young. My fear of cats, in particular, is the result of an unfortunate experience I prefer not to speak about."

"I hope you will tell me about it one day."

"Don't get your hopes up. Certain family secrets should remain buried."

"You seem to be bearing a heavy burden on your shoulders."

"Is that not the lot of every heir? I must join the family business and prepare to take over from my father."

"No one is a prisoner of his destiny."

Vincent blinked as he gazed at Penny, as if he were dazzled by bright light. His cheeks were ablaze, and for a brief moment, he reminded me of the child he once was – the boy who had not yet learned to temper his enthusiasm and restrain his ardour. But then his face clouded over as quickly as it had brightened.

"Don't say that to my mother! She is already convinced I will be the ruin of the Delormes. She believes in the curse of family fortunes: the first generation accumulates the capital, the second profits from the interest, while the third quickly fritters it away."

"Do you intend to burn through your inheritance?"

"Money is a form of servitude I would prefer to avoid."

"You must first free yourself from your secrets."

"Even the most shameful ones?"

"I fear you must."

This time, nothing could stop Vincent from smiling.

"If I were to confide in someone, it would not be anyone but you."

How sweet those two were. But it was high time for them to stop speaking with such ridiculous formality.

1949

It was midnight when Morula, Gastrula, and Blastula burst into little Vincent's room and switched on the ceiling fixture. Its blinding light wrested him pitilessly from his peaceful sleep. They warned him not to say a word, blindfolded him, and led him down to the basement. In single file, they crossed the kitchen and the laundry room, guided by the muffled, threatening roar of the furnace.

When his bare feet touched the cold concrete floor, the boy realized they had entered the coal cellar, a place he had always been forbidden to go on pain of punishment most dire. Too terrified to retreat, he tried to catch a glimpse of what awaited him through the opening in his blindfold. All he could distinguish was a narrow door made of a single panel of tempered steel with neither hinges nor handle, and blackened by long tongues of soot. He was about to hazard a question when an ear-splitting squeal shattered the silence. The door, powered by some unknown force, swung open, suffusing the coal-saturated air with the headiest perfume imaginable: that of freshly printed banknotes. The women shoved Vincent through the opening, and three steps later, tore the blindfold from his eyes.

There he beheld, in the light of the torches, the life-sized portrait of King George VI. Then he spotted the cupola of the former root cellar, with its mosaic of oxidized copper coins, and the walls painted in that green so familiar to numismatists – which, of all colours, is the most pleasing to the eye, for it is the exact complement to blood red. His gaze came to rest on the pyramid that rose from the centre of the room, all the more impressive for being built from sheaves of greenbacks, carefully stacked and bound by the kinds of rubber bands used by letter carriers. The boy quickly calculated that there must have been no less than two hundred thousand dollars stored in this vault. How many years, and how many sacrifices, had it taken to amass such a sum?

Lost in his calculations, for a moment Vincent forgot the dangers that hung over his head. But the feeling of dread returned when he saw his mother and father. Both were attired in full-length albs whose murky glow was reflected on their skin, making Estelle appear even more reptilian than usual. Stepping toward her son, she made him lie face down on the floor in front of the portrait of the King.

"Prostrate yourself before His Majesty."

With papal solemnity, Louis-Dollard took up a position behind the pyramid. He was holding a clay brick, which he elevated above his head like a host.

"We convene tonight in the Green Chamber to receive Vincent into our order," he intoned. "This new vocation is a great source of pride for the Delorme family, but it is also a great duty for the novice who joins it tonight. Vincent, you must now swear to henceforth serve the Mother Coin, defend the integrity of the Family Treasury, and contribute to its growth your whole life long. By virtue of the dignity of your sacrifice, you hereby agree to submit, body and soul, to the supreme authority of Capital and forgo the benefits of its interests. The better to honour your vows and uphold your pledge, you will resist, day in and day out, the temptation to spend, and never keep in your pocket more than you absolutely need."

With the full authority vested in him as celebrant, he commanded Vincent to rise and approach him.

"Now, repeat after me this prayer."

> *Our Dollar who art so precious*
> *Hallowed be Thy worth*
> *May Thy savings come*
> *And Thy profits grow in our pockets and our coffers.*
> *Give us this day our daily interest*
> *And forgive us our expenses*
> *As we never forgive a single debt.*
> *Lead us not into speculation,*
> *But deliver us from ruin.*
> *Amen!*

"By this sacred brick that holds the Mother Coin and upon which is founded our church, I bless you. In the name of the Dollar, the Cent, and the Holy Economy!"

Vincent's aunts gathered around him while Estelle, as chief of ceremonies, handed the officiant a jar containing pine tar, which he applied to the lad's hands so that "money may never slip between his fingers." Then he gave him a small piggy bank made of translucent plastic with a slit on top into which he inserted a copper, a nickel, and a silver coin.

"Receive this piggy bank, the emblem of your entry into Holy Orders, and with it, three coins that, like magnets, will attract all others to them. Henceforth a member of the Order of His Majesty and guardian of his secrets, you are sworn to silence. Should ever you reveal to anyone the amount of our fortune or the existence of the Green Chamber, know that you will be brought before our tribunal and punished with the utmost severity."

He then replaced the blindfold over the eyes of his petrified son, and the sisters returned him to his bed.

Vincent spent the rest of the night staring wide-eyed into the darkness.

When Louis-Dollard first spoke of his intention to give the boy money, Estelle strongly opposed the decision.

"He will only lose it or spend it."

But Louis-Dollard held firm.

"If he has no money, how will he learn to save?"

Anxious to demonstrate the wisdom of his decision, he showed Vincent how to fill out a deposit slip and handed him a bank book so that he would always know his balance – which, for the time being, stood at sixteen cents. He introduced him to the basics of the liturgy, and explained the difference between a capital and a material sin, and had him memorize the order's Ten Commandments:

1. *Thou shalt have no other god than His Majesty.*
2. *Thou shalt honour the Mother Coin and all other denominations and never destroy them.*
3. *Thou shalt remember that money grows not on trees.*
4. *Thou shalt keep no small change upon thyself.*
5. *Thou shalt not spend in vain.*
6. *Thou shalt give naught to the poor.*
7. *Thou shalt make no loan, nor engage in pawn nor usury.*
8. *Thou shalt not gamble.*
9. *Thou shalt not accept counterfeit money.*
10. *Thou shalt not covet the goods sold in stores.*

Finally, before letting him go, he repeated the wise truth that his own father had passed down to him.

"Scrape as you might, you will never reach the bottom of your needs."

For a whole year, Vincent was content to admire his fortune through the pink plastic fog of the piggy bank, and his father congratulated himself for having shown such confidence in his son. But there came a day when, as he was shaking the piggy bank to hear the clink of the coins, one of them became stuck in the slot. Curiosity got the better of him, and he gave it a sharp pull.

For the first time in his life, Vincent held a genuine coin in his hand, and could examine it at leisure. The penny was not new; it was as dark as the inside of a safe. Despite the heavy patina and wear from years of use, the double maple leaf motif that flanked the year 1923 and, on the obverse, the noble profile of George V and "Dei Gratia Rex et Indiae Imperator" were still prominent enough to be visible. Vincent hefted the coin in his hand, rolled it across the floor, and certified empirically that its surface could indeed contain thirty drops of water. He was enjoying himself so thoroughly that when it came time to replace the coin in the piggy bank, he hesitated. What harm could possibly come from keeping it on his person a while longer? After all, the coin would remain securely in his pocket …

He went out and his steps led him to the station, which at that hour of the afternoon was deserted. Turning his eyes toward Mount Royal, he spotted the three o'clock train emerging from the tunnel. In four minutes, it would come to a stop at the platform. An impulse as inexplicable as it was irresistible rose up in him. Forgetting the second commandment, and without considering the consequences of his act, he jumped down onto the tracks and placed his penny on one of the rails. Then he sat down on the weedy embankment and waited. As the train approached, he saw the coin begin to vibrate, then vanish beneath the wheels as the brakes screeched and the locomotive came to a halt. Several ladies detrained, and as no one was boarding, the conductor gave the departure signal to the engineer. Vincent waited prudently until the last car had passed before climbing down to the tracks. What he found on the ballast no longer resembled a penny. It was a copper disc as flat as a piece of paper.

The experience should have taught him a lesson. But a month later, he began to fiddle with his piggy bank again, this time inserting a letter opener in the slot until he was able to extract the five-cent piece. As well as featuring the effigy of a beaver, his favourite animal, the coin bore the date 1939 – the year of his birth. When he went out to play, he made sure not to stray beyond the boundaries of the property. It was the day after a snowstorm, and the coin slipped from his hands and dropped into the snow. He searched everywhere but could not find his nickel.

"What are you looking for?" called Morula, opening the window from which she had been observing him.

Vincent had to invent a story.

"I lost one of my mittens."

"Don't waste your time, you'll never see it again. When the snow melts in the spring, your mitten will be carried deep beneath the earth, and will come to the surface in China."

All that remained in the piggy bank was the silver dime, depicting the racing schooner *Bluenose*. Curious to learn what the coin could buy, Vincent set off on a tour of the small businesses that occupied the centre of the Enclave. He walked past the barbershop, Clément's shoe repair with its little cans of polish in all colours, and Monsieur Vachon's shop for new shoes, where pink slippers for little girls taking ballet lessons were lined up in the window. He went into Taylor's, an ill-kept establishment that sold soft drinks, cigarettes, and sweets. It was a paradise of chocolate bars, wax flutes, pointed lollipops, sponge toffee squares, licorice sticks, honey drops, pepsin gum, caramels, and candy apples. Standing in front of the counter, Vincent felt no pleasure – only queasiness. His lost look awakened distrust in Mrs. Taylor, who suspected all children of wanting to steal the merchandise.

"What do you want?" she asked in approximate French. "Bubble gum?"

Intimidated, Vincent stepped up to the counter. Next to the

cash register sat a small yellow coin box on which was written, "Support the Oratory's Good Works." He dropped the ten-cent piece into the slot and left the store relieved and enchanted.

ည

Vincent slept more peacefully after relieving himself of his fortune: no more nightmares, no more guilty conscience, and no more insomnia. He was still a light sleeper, however, and less than a week later, he was awakened by the squeaking of the door hinges. Someone had slipped into his room by night – a ghostly figure in a long white gown that gave off a sweet odour. As the silhouette passed in front of his window, Vincent recognized the aquiline profile of his aunt Morula.

She had just put away a bottle of vanilla extract and had no money to purchase more. In desperation, she hoped to purloin Vincent's sixteen cents without anyone noticing. She felt her way through the room until her hands encountered the distinctive contours of the piggy bank. She picked up the little plastic animal, shook it, and then had to face the facts: it was empty!

That would be the end of it, Vincent believed. But next morning, he was summoned to his father's office. Rarely was he admitted into the paternal sanctuary, and never for any positive reason. This time, he knew what to expect. He tapped timidly on the door. Louis-Dollard was seated in his swivel chair, Estelle standing erect beside him, with the three aunts drawn up behind them. There could be no doubt: court was in session, the jury was seated in the jury box, and the incriminating evidence stood in full view on the desk.

Using his preferred method of intimidation, Louis-Dollard left the lad standing there for a good five minutes before speaking to him.

"I seem to recall that I gave you a penny, a nickel, and a

128

dime, which is more than a boy your age should have in the first place. Now there is nothing left in your piggy bank. What happened to your money?"

"I misplaced it."

"Then you must confess. And I caution you not to tell us any tall stories, for you will be lying only to yourself."

Vincent gathered his courage and admitted he had lost the smallest denominations.

"And the ten-cent coin?"

"I disposed of it."

"Will you please repeat what you just said? I believe I've misunderstood."

Vincent gulped so loudly he was afraid the whole household had heard.

"I gave it to a charitable cause," he finally admitted in a choked voice.

"Charity." Of all the words in the language, none was so loathed by the Delormes.

"I told you he was too young to be trusted with money," hissed Estelle.

"When the prodigal son returns to the family hearth, it is time to kill the fatted calf," said Louis-Dollard. "Gastrula, go down to the Green Chamber and kindle the brazier."

ꙮ

Louis-Dollard cast three coins onto the burning coals and told Vincent, "Hold out your hands, beggar boy."

Picking up the incandescent pennies with a small pair of tongs, he dropped them onto the lad's open palms. Vincent let out a piteous and heart-rending wail.

"Now you know what happens when money burns your fingers."

Vincent stared horrified at his hand. Blisters of pus had begun to form.

"You will have not one cent more until you reach the age of majority," said Louis-Dollard. "Consider yourself fortunate that you have not been disinherited."

1963

E stelle awoke sensing a strange animal presence in her bed. She sat bolt upright. There, in Louis-Dollard's place, was a large rectangular box stamped with gold-embossed script: "Salon Laura Boucher." Unhappy at being awakened, she unceremoniously ripped off the top. Among the folds of delicate tissue paper appeared a sheared beaver coat of oyster hue with silver highlights, fastened with three rhinestone buttons and bearing the initials "ED" embroidered on its satin lining.

"What new folly awaits us now?" she exclaimed as she threw back the bedclothes. "Champagne and diamonds?"

The fur was as smooth as velvet and from it rose the discreet scent of luxury, were a person to put her nose to it. Despite its volume, the coat was as light as a feather, and Estelle, covetousness dilating her pupils, could not resist the temptation to slip it on once she completed her toilette. As she went past the mirror, she noticed it suited her far better than her mouse-fur stole, and she paused a moment to admire herself from every possible angle, whistling softly. Would vanity get the better of her?

That morning, she firmly intended to take the household in hand, and the first order of business was to march downstairs to the office and carry out a full audit of the family accounts. What she found was devastating: nearly one thousand dollars was missing from the strongbox, and the books did not balance. She immediately summoned Vincent and presented an accurate and unvarnished description of the financial abyss into which Louis-Dollard had cast them.

"It is now up to you to do your duty and save us from this mess. Expedients are no longer enough. You must ask for Penny's hand this very day. Without her dowry, we are finished."

She expected Vincent to slump into his chair by way of acquiescence. But, with a nonchalance as strange as it was unexpected, he tossed his pencil onto the desk and, stretching out his arms and lacing his fingers, ostentatiously cracked his knuckles. His bold demeanour lent him a self-assurance that I never would have suspected from him.

"Miss Sterling is an admirable young lady. She certainly deserves better than to be exploited for her fortune."

"Are you forgetting that in exchange she will enjoy the privilege of bearing our name?"

"Our feelings for each other are still, for the moment, of a strictly friendly nature."

"One must never rely on one's emotions, my boy, particularly when it comes to laying down the foundations of a marriage of convenience."

"I beg to differ."

Estelle did not appreciate the change in her son's attitude. She appreciated even less the challenge to her authority.

"I don't know what has gotten into you, but you have become too big for your britches. I warn you that in these circumstances I will not tolerate the slightest insubordination."

"With all due respect, I will not give an inch on the fundamental principle of reciprocal love."

"We shall see about that."

She turned up the collar of her beaver coat and stormed out of the office.

Head high, bosom puffed out like a wineskin, she burst into the garage. Spying Louis-Dollard sulking behind the workbench, she beckoned to him to stand up.

"Put on your cap," she commanded. "We're going for a drive."

The sight of his wife swaddled in the gift he had given her buoyed Louis-Dollard's hopes of rapprochement. He rushed to open the rear door for Estelle and then sat down behind the wheel. And off they went, like a liveried chauffeur and his lady. From time to time he glanced in the rear-view mirror in hopes of catching Estelle's eye and so confirm her indulgence. But she was still irritated by the conversation with Vincent, and her expression was sullen. The vasodilation of her blotchy complexion lent her a purplish hue that was threatening to turn violet. They circled the park several times before she deigned to speak to him.

"Did you really think you could appease me with a fur coat?"

"Well, a gift is not necessarily something that one deserves, but that one must gratefully accept ..."

"Whom do you take me for? Never would I yield to such a flagrant attempt at corruption."

"There, there, Estelle ... After all, you are hardly above baseness and venality yourself."

"Whatever the case, be advised that I will pardon you only when Vincent is officially engaged."

The motor chose that moment to misfire, and before it quit entirely, Louis-Dollard headed for home. He deposited Estelle on the front porch.

Then he turned to her, and asked timidly, "If you don't want the coat, may I return it to the shop so I can get my money back?"

By way of answer, Estelle slammed the door in his face.

ตฒ

Louis-Dollard was a little disappointed by the day's events, but not excessively discouraged. It would not be too difficult, he believed, to convince Vincent to marry. Penny Sterling was not only a good catch when it came to her resources, she had a pleasant personality and was, what's more, very attractive. In his son's position, he wouldn't waste a second. Full of confidence, he went to see Vincent in his room.

"Son, I can't keep from you the fact that I'm in dire straits. My absurd situation cannot go on much longer. Negotiate though I may with your mother, she is totally inflexible."

Vincent squirmed in his chair, unable to conceal his discomfort. He had no desire to be caught up in his parents' quarrels.

"Are you asking me to intercede on your behalf?"

"That would be futile. I'm afraid that all the resources of diplomacy would not be enough to weaken Estelle's resolve. She has made my return conditional on one thing: your engagement. Son, my fate is in your hands."

Vincent rolled up his sleeves and clenched his fists.

"Filial duty has its limits, and they have been well and truly exceeded. Your plan regarding Miss Sterling is ignoble, and I refuse to be a part of it."

"Don't make any hasty decisions. Listen first to my proposal. You have much to gain, I promise you. In exchange for your cooperation, I am prepared to share our family's most precious secret: the combination to the Green Chamber."

"No, thank you. I have no desire to enter that cursed place."

"Be careful, my boy. Your words border on heresy."

"If I ever had the faith of my ancestors, I renounce it. I have begged you to strike my name from your will, and you have always refused. It is pointless to pursue this sterile discussion."

Faced with the prospect of ending his days in the garage, Louis-Dollard's cunning took over.

"Agree to become engaged to her and I will disinherit you!"

His words left Vincent so stunned, he couldn't move. Who could blame him for succumbing so fast to the feeling of lightness that filled him at the thought of being freed of the millstone that had hung from his neck since birth? His breathing, normally shallow, grew even as the stiffness lifted from his shoulders, and an unaccustomed serenity welled up in him. His vacillation did not escape Louis-Dollard.

"I knew you would listen to reason. I will inform your mother of the good news."

ಬಜ

Light footed, Louis-Dollard swanned down the hall and entered Estelle's room. The sight of the conjugal bed filled him with nostalgia. He would have given anything to recline there, if only for an instant, and lay his worried head on the soft pillow. But his wife was displaying signs of impatience, and he needed to move fast.

"Everything is arranged," he said, not without a certain pride at succeeding where she had failed.

Estelle rubbed her hands, seeing that her efforts had at last met with success.

"We cannot rely on Vincent to take the initiative," she said. "Better I get involved, and the sooner the better. I shall invite Penny this noon. It is a beautiful day, and a picnic in the garden will be the ideal occasion to cement the betrothal."

"Do you intend to do it yourself?" asked Louis-Dollard apprehensively.

"Of course not. I will feign a dizzy spell and withdraw at the most opportune moment. But I will observe operations from my window, and should Vincent appear to retreat, I will not hesitate to intervene. What time is it?"

"Quarter to ten."

"There's no time to lose. I'll go down to the kitchen and give Gastrula her instructions. Blastula will set up the table in the garden. In the meantime, make yourself useful and repair that damned automobile. It made so much noise this morning I was dreadfully ashamed of what the neighbours would think."

Louis-Dollard refrained from questioning orders issued in such a peremptory tone. He went back to the garage, only too happy to escape the overheated atmosphere that pervaded the household. He propped open the hood of the car, turned on the motor, and got to work. But he was no expert mechanic and could not determine the nature of the problem. As he was checking whether the fan belt was slipping, I thought of the problems that would arise should Estelle's plans succeed. Vincent was my only hope. I had been waiting for years for him to become head of the family so I could return to my original lustre. In all conscience, I could not allow Louis-Dollard to disinherit him. That would be the end of me. The opportunity that was about to arise might never come again. It was so unhoped for that I could only interpret it as the mark of destiny. Would I dare seize the hour?

I whispered a final prayer for Louis-Dollard, who was soon to fall asleep, never to reawaken. But I felt neither sorrow nor pity when I dropped the counterweight of the garage door and silently brought it down.

1954

There was a time, not long ago, when Estelle would never have let Vincent out of her sight. She watched over him night and day, noting down the time he spent in the shower and insisting that his door be kept open, even when he was changing clothes. She allowed her son no form of privacy and considered any attempt at withdrawal an act of rebellion. Even at age fifteen, he was not permitted to get out of bed in the morning until his mother had first inspected the sheets.

"It's a crime to squander one's seed," she reminded him with pleasure when she detected a tiny drop of nocturnal pollution, as though her son had knowingly engaged in self-abuse.

Convinced that humiliation would put an end to such filth, she encircled the spot with red topstitching and dispatched Vincent to hang the sheet on the clothesline so the neighbours could witness his shame. A year later, the sheet resembled a patchwork quilt, but replacing it was out of the question, for that would have created a dangerous precedent. Vincent was never given permission to discard his worn-out clothing. His trousers were too short, his shirt collars frayed, and even the thickest application of polish could not disguise the pitiful state of his shoes. The boy looked so neglected that the school monitor in charge of discipline sent his parents a written complaint.

"*If the dress of this student does not improve in short order,*" he concluded, "*we will be obliged to take corrective action.*"

His threats fell on deaf ears, since nothing could convince

Estelle that a young person, unable to appreciate the price of clothing, deserved anything more than rags.

Vincent's appearance didn't help make him popular with his schoolmates, who tended to exclude him from their games, and never invited him to their homes. He could only listen as they talked of their outings, their skiing holidays, their horseback riding, their weekends in the country – and though all these activities were foreign to him, he had no difficulty imagining the pleasure associated with them, and that he could have derived from them, had he not been forced to spend his Saturdays in the library, an activity strongly encouraged because it was free.

It was on those shelves of books, which he idly perused out of boredom, that Vincent made a discovery that was to change his life: the Trailblazer novel series with its high-spirited adventure tales that sang the praises of scouting. He couldn't join the heroes of those pages, the Wolf Pack or the Daredevils, so our heir apparent asked to be admitted into the parish scout troop that met in the church basement. Estelle strongly opposed letting her son join an organization that promoted mutual assistance and required its members to solemnly promise to "help others, whatever the cost." But since Vincent did not have to purchase his uniform or the used equipment passed on to him by a former scout, Louis-Dollard gave his permission. During his stay at camp, which that year was held on the banks of a river in the Laurentians, Vincent experienced life outside the family cocoon for the first time. Not only did he learn how to build a fire, swim, paddle a canoe, and find his way in the woods with a compass, he also made a friend.

The boy's name was Julian, and his family was among the most recent arrivals in the Enclave. They had moved into an immense Spanish-style house on Rockland Avenue, with stucco walls and a red-tile roof, which the Delormes, in their customary disdain for the flashy displays favoured by the nouveaux riches, described as a "white elephant." Vincent knew that his parents would never allow him to set foot there, so he told his mother he would be spending the afternoon at the library the day Julian invited him to visit. Rockland Avenue was a good ten minutes from his house. He covered the distance in five. He arrived out of breath at his friend's house and paused a moment to admire the fire-engine red Studebaker Champion convertible parked in the crescent driveway. Julian opened the wrought-iron front door.

"You didn't bring your swimsuit?" he said. "No problem. I'll lend you one of mine."

As he crossed the entrance hall, Vincent was dazzled by the polished terrazzo flooring where, as though in a mirror, the thousand lights of an immense chandelier were reflected. They passed through an ultramodern kitchen, finished with chrome and shiny laminate, then went downstairs into a large room Julian called the "den." It was a cave carpeted with a geometric-patterned rug, whose centrepiece was a Zenith television with a bulbous screen set into a massive walnut cabinet. Comfortably seated in a leather armchair with a glass of Scotch on the rocks in his hand, Julian's father was watching a football game so intently that he offered only a perfunctory greeting to the two boys. They opened the sliding glass door and stepped into the yard – and there, miracle of miracles, stood an in-ground swimming pool whose shimmering turquoise water could not have been more inviting. Julian handed Vincent a swimsuit.

"Change in the cabin and come join me."

So it was that Vincent spent his day diving into the water, floating on the air mattress and eating ice cream, playing Mille Bornes, and watching cartoons on television. At five o'clock Julian's mother made her entrance, arms laden with packages. She had come from the shopping centre, where she had bought dresses and perfume. As she took off her half-veil and white gloves, she turned to Vincent.

"You'll be having dinner with us, won't you?"

How could our heir refuse such an invitation, especially since it came from such a youthful, beautiful, and glamorous woman? Docilely, he took a seat at the dining table, where the plates had been set atop shiny vinyl placemats. His amazement grew in intensity as dish after dish appeared in front of him. First he was served a bowl of chicken-noodle soup made from a mix, and then, for the first time in his life, he tasted canned ravioli. Desert was an angel-food cake with marshmallow frosting that had been bought at Woolworth's. He found the meal all the more delicious, for nothing was homemade.

Then came the fateful moment when Julian's father got up from the table and offered to drive him home. It is as if I can still see our heir disembark with infinite caution from the Studebaker, his face fallen; an escapee would not have been more reluctant to return to his prison cell. I would have opened the door for him had Louis-Dollard not been waiting for him in the hall, blocking his way with the full breadth of his barrel chest. It was as if he did not recognize his own son.

"Since you have not respected the schedule we drew up for you, you will have to find another rooming house for the night. Clear out now or I'll call the police."

The door swung shut and the light in the vestibule went dark. The verdict had come down, and it was irreversible. Vincent would have to sleep outside. He paced back and forth on the front porch, hoping that his father, moved by compassion, would change his mind. He lost that hope as the night began to grow cold. I tried to keep him warm and ease his sobbing as he curled up against my foundations. I was mortified by my inability to offer consolation, but what else could I do for him?

ༀༀ

A family council was held the next day, during which Vincent's case was discussed as an urgent matter. All agreed that he had

taken a dangerous turn, and several solutions were suggested –
the most radical being to lock him up in reform school until
he reached the age of maturity, since it was impossible to enrol
him in the army. Louis-Dollard reminded his wife and his sisters
that sloth was the mother of all vices, and that the boy simply
did not have enough to keep himself busy. Happily, the voice
of reason prevailed, and it was unanimously decided that he be
put to work – in the service and in the interests of the Delorme
family, of course.

So it was that our heir apparent became an employee of the
family business, the apprentice janitor of our apartment building.
Every morning, before going off to school, he had to attend to a
long list of tasks: polish the handrails and letter boxes, wash the
hall floors, replace the burnt-out bulbs, sweep out the garages,
unplug the blocked drains, repair the leaky faucets, replace the
electric elements in the stoves. In good weather he mowed the
lawns and finished the edges with shears, pulled dandelions and
turned over the compost. When it rained, he made the inventory
of the workshop where the motors and spare oil pumps for the
furnaces were stored, along with the electrical supplies, plumbing,
and venetian blinds. After a snowstorm in the night, he awoke
at dawn to shovel the driveways and sidewalks ...

He displayed such diligence that Louis-Dollard entrusted
him with the weighty responsibility of managing the revenues
from the coin-operated washing machines in the building's
laundry room. Every Thursday Vincent deposited the dimes
in a sheepskin mitten, counted them out, and rolled them in
paper tubes, which were then deposited in the old tackle box
that held the petty cash.

The bottom of the box was lined with a parchment paper
document. One day, Vincent mustered the curiosity to unfold it:
he discovered his grandfather Prosper's last will and testament.

When he read the codicil, he understood he had a cousin
whose existence had been hidden from him – a poor orphan

who had been deprived of his inheritance and who now lived, in all likelihood, in the most abject poverty. He imagined him begging on a street corner, pale, sad, tubercular, dressed in rags, chilled to the bone. Had his parents really committed the shameful act of robbing that child of his comfort and security, his very future? He thought of the banknotes stacked up in the Green Chamber and pictured them drenched with innocent blood. He swore on the spot that he would find his cousin and obtain reparations for him, with interest, for all the evil the Delormes had inflicted upon him.

৯৫৯

One fine autumn morning, as Vincent was raking the dead leaves that had fallen from the Manitoba maple, Louis-Dollard came up to him and laid a paternal hand on his shoulder.

"Put down your rake," he said. "Today I'm taking you big-game hunting."

Gunny sacks at the ready, they took up position in the alley behind a row of garbage cans.

"What are we waiting for?" Vincent asked after twenty minutes had passed.

His father motioned to him to keep quiet, for a reddish cat was approaching. Vincent knew the animal: it was poor Darcy, which Miss Keaton had taken in half-dead from hunger. She brought him back to life, rid him of his fleas, and even had him vaccinated at the veterinarian's. The cat was the apple of her eye.

Drawn by the tempting smells of refuse, Darcy came up to the garbage cans and began to sniff appreciatively. At that very moment, Louis-Dollard jumped on the cat and threw the gunny sack over him.

"Let's get back to the house before someone spots us," he said, holding the sack away from his body as the cat mewed plaintively inside.

He led his son down into the furnace room and ordered him to light the garbage incinerator.

"Our tenant had the nerve to take in a cat, when it clearly stipulates in Article 53 of the lease, which she duly signed, that domestic animals are forbidden in our apartments! She'll see soon enough what we're made of."

In the sack, Darcy had recovered his original wild state. He twisted and turned violently and his mewing turned into howls of rage.

"Go ahead!" said Louis-Dollard. "You have the honour of stoking the fire!"

Pushed by his father, Vincent had no choice but to cast the gunny sack into the flames.

"Now close the grate, otherwise he'll escape."

Vincent was petrified. His eyes were fixed on the burnt offering and he didn't even feel the tears flowing down his cheeks. The shrieking of the cat echoed in the chimney as a pungent stench rose from his roasting flesh, then all that could be heard was the crackle of his bones as his skeleton collapsed into the coals.

"Your mother will be amused when Miss Keaton starts calling for her lost cat," said Louis-Dollard. "And as for you, son, you have earned a small reward."

In a burst of generosity, he handed Vincent a new banknote.

"It displays the likeness of our new sovereign, Queen Elizabeth II, whose coronation was celebrated last year. Keep it preciously."

The green bill with a face value of one dollar was issued in Ottawa in 1954 and bore the serial number FD8593322, as well as the signatures of Messrs. Beattie and Coyne, respectively deputy governor and governor of the Bank of Canada. The coat of arms and the motto of the country were integrated into the background, and on the right half of the bill Her Majesty was depicted in a satin gown bedecked with diamonds. Her face bore a frozen expression. The waves of her hair, however, appeared strangely alive. Due to a bizarre syndrome known as pareidolia that can cause us to perceive human traits in inanimate objects, Vincent suddenly spotted the face of a grinning devil in the Queen's curls. He cried out and dropped the banknote; it had inflicted tiny lacerations on his fingers.

From then on in his mind, he had no doubt: all evils flowed from money – it was the very root of Evil itself.

1963

A fantastic dumping ground: no other words could describe Louis-Dollard's backyard. The porch, an assemblage of rotten planks and broken bricks, was so uneven a person could hardly venture onto it without spraining an ankle. In the centre, a wheelbarrow served as a basin, and its fetid waters rivalled the stench of the compost heap fermenting in the far corner. In the flower beds, at two-foot intervals, my venerable founder had planted a handful of sickly-looking velvet pulmonaria, all of which had grown from the rhizomes of a single plant and chosen for the minimal care they required. From the branches of a viburnum stripped of its leaves by snails, he had suspended a cheap version of wind chimes: five cracked clay pots that, at the slightest breath of wind, would rattle against each other, producing a hollow clank.

Could there have been a more inhospitable place for a garden party? Yet it was there that Estelle had set up the rusty card table and, lacking a plastic tablecloth, covered it with a mildewed shower curtain. She made a greater effort by placing, at various strategic locations, three mirrors that would let her monitor the billing and cooing of the lovebirds from the window where she would be positioned. That task accomplished, she stepped back to admire the perspective. She had to concede it presented a sorry spectacle. The platter of radish sandwiches Gastrula prepared hardly enlivened the situation – and would certainly not encourage the kind of impulse that brings human beings together and leads them naturally toward the common ground of intimacy – without realizing that the trap of engagement was about to snap closed around them.

Forced by necessity, in spite of her miserliness, Estelle set out to make a few purchases. As she stepped onto the sidewalk, she felt the onset of vertigo. A good ten years had passed since she last ventured beyond the bounds of our property alone, and she needed added impetus to continue. At first, her confinement was voluntary, since she believed that outings of any kind inevitably contributed to expenses, while it cost nothing to remain in the comfort of her home. Little by little, her world began to shrink, and as it grew smaller, the outside began to appear to her as strange as it was hostile. From my walls, which should have provided refuge, she fashioned a dungeon, and she emerged from it with some anxiety. It took all her courage to reach Madame Rosita's pastry shop, located just at the corner.

She entered with the firm intention to leave with the least expensive item in the shop. But her scruples melted like sugar in the sun when the rich smell of croissants and fresh-baked bread reached her nostrils, and her colour, drained from her face by anxiety, slowly crept back to her cheeks. She moved past the refrigerated display case where cakes, petits fours, meringues, and marzipan figurines were exhibited and she came to a stop, swooning, before the array of pastries: cream puffs, chocolate eclairs, rum babas, coffee religieuses, strawberry tartlets, lemon barquettes, small frosted mice, carrot cakes with coconut icing, and napoleons in mouth-watering varieties.

While she was trying to make up her mind, a little girl entered and walked up to the cash. She was wearing a pretty dress in the Black Watch tartan with lace cuffs and collar, but her pixie haircut lent her the miserable look of a child of the streets. Madame Rosita welcomed her with a wide smile and handed her a shortbread topped with a candied cherry.

"This is for you," she said in her thick Spanish accent. "Now go back to your mommy."

Estelle called to the pastry mistress and with a stunning lack of courtesy asked, "Can I try one too?"

Quite surprised, Madame Rosita handed her a piece of shortbread. Estelle popped it whole into her mouth and let it melt on her tongue. The pleasure that the flavours of butter, sugar, and vanilla procured were equalled only by having obtained something for free.

"What can I do for you?" asked Madame Rosita, shaking her curly black hair, revealing the sheen of two golden earrings.

"A dozen French pastries!"

Madame Rosita located her metal tongs and selected an assortment of her specialties, which she arranged in a white cardboard box closed with a tightly knotted ribbon.

"That will be three dollars, plus five cents for the shortbread," she said, entering the amount on the cash register.

Estelle rummaged through her change purse and paid without thinking twice. What did it matter? she thought. These excessive expenses would soon be over – just a bad memory once she pocketed Penny's fortune.

ഇരു

Package in hand, she left the pastry shop with an almost spritely step, pressing her nose to the opening in the box to capture the emanations of its contents. As she passed by the garage she heard the sound of the motor. She was so satisfied to see that Louis-Dollard was hard at work repairing the car that she paid no heed to the closed door – thank God.

The thought of Vincent, true enough, weighed on her mind, for his slovenly dress was totally inappropriate for a declaration of such magnitude. She hurried upstairs to her son's room and pulled his old college uniform from the closet: grey flannel trousers and a crested blue marine blazer. She added one of

Louis-Dollard's ties to the ensemble – the grey silk one with tiny red polka dots that always makes me think of a speckled trout.

She also brought a jewel box lined with green velvet. She handed it to Vincent along with several recommendations.

"Here, this will help you conclude the transaction. This is family jewellery I intend to keep, so I am only lending it to you. After you are married, I will retrieve it."

Vincent was less concerned with what Penny might think of his taste in clothes than how she might judge his heredity.

"How can I convince her I'm not like them?" he whispered to himself when Estelle finally left him. "How I wish I had been adopted!"

He hung the blazer and the trousers in the closet and threw the tie on the bed, choosing to stay in short sleeves and loafers. He had not shaved and avoided pleasing his mother by drawing a comb through his hair. Before slipping the green velvet jewel box into his pocket, he opened it and saw a diamond ring in a cathedral setting with white-gold filigree. He gazed at the brilliant with its two baguettes, which gleamed with the duplicity of thirty pieces of silver. Was the reward of having his name struck from a will really worth soiling his heart with the vilest of treachery? I would have whispered the answer to him, but the decision was his and his alone.

ಬಾ

When he finally decided to go down to the backyard, he found Penny perched on the low wall, her delicate, shapely legs swinging back and forth. He looked toward the table and spotted the tray of radish sandwiches and the pastries still in their cardboard box.

"I hope my mother's schemes haven't tricked you," he told Penny in a most familiar tone. "All this is part of her wretched efforts at playing marriage broker."

"Not to worry. I saw through her little game from the very beginning, and I'm quite capable of defending myself."

"I don't doubt it, but I'm afraid you might underestimate my parents' rapacity. Ever since they learned the amount of your fortune, all they can think about is getting hold of it and, believe me, they're ready to do anything to achieve their ends – even corrupting their own son. This very morning, my father promised to disinherit me if I agreed to ask for your hand."

"What a curious way to buy someone …"

"He knows I would be only too happy never to touch his cursed pile of money."

"Your integrity does you honour."

"This situation is as embarrassing for me as it is for you. You are under no obligation to stay, but before you go, there are two things I would like to say."

"Go ahead, I'm listening."

With a swift kick, Vincent sent a pebble skittering off down the path.

"I'm troubled by something that concerns you – so troubled that I don't know where to start."

"Well, try starting at the beginning."

"I came upon something in the ledger that puts me in a difficult position …"

"Go on."

"I tried to cover up the matter, and say nothing to my mother, but I'm afraid I won't be able to fool her much longer. Do you see what I'm getting at?"

Penny swung her legs back and forth with splendid nonchalance.

"Oh, you must be talking about the rent I haven't paid for several months now."

"It's not the kind of oversight my parents take lightly, and I'm afraid it might cause you trouble …"

Penny shrugged her shoulders.

"I have a confession to make. I rented the apartment using a fake bank book. I never invented any game, I have no income – in fact, I don't have a red cent to my name."

Vincent dropped onto a bench when he realized she wasn't joking. I had not seen him laugh very much during the long years of our shared existence, but now he burst into great peals of joy.

"What irony!" he said once he caught his breath. "It would serve my parents right if we got engaged, just to teach them a lesson!"

With a grand sweep of her arms, she leaped down from the wall and landed right under Vincent's nose. She looked into his eyes, and their cheeks almost touched as she whispered into his ear.

"I accept."

Emboldened by Penny's saucy self-assurance, he thrust his hand into his pocket, pulled out the green velvet box, and handed it to her. She drew back when she saw the circular scars on his palms.

"What happened to your hands?"

Vincent began nervously plucking leaves from the viburnum.

"Another secret I'll tell you one day."

Penny lifted the lid discreetly, as the circumstances demanded. At the sight of the diamonds gleaming in the sun, her eyes filled with tears, though they were neither tears of joy nor emotion. I cannot explain why, but she seemed to be crying with bitterness. Yes, that was it: a bitterness blurred by hate distorted her pretty face.

Vincent saw none of that, for as he was about to slip the ring onto her finger, he caught sight of the glare from a mirror hidden in the pulmonaria bush and in it, the image of his mother spying on them from her window.

"Let's not stay here," he whispered, leading his new friend toward the gate. "I know a place that's far from prying eyes."

꩜

A swarm of wasps broke the new silence of the backyard. Drawn by the sugar, the little rascals descended upon the pastries, swooping low over the blobs of whipped cream with a hum and thrusting their articulated legs into the layers of frosting. Their depredations did not escape Estelle, who bolted panic stricken from her room and hurried down the stairs as fast as her ample girth would allow. Arms akimbo, she rushed outside, dispatched the wasps with a wave, and snatched up the box of pastries, which she clutched jealously to her flabby midriff.

She was fully prepared to sacrifice her booty to avoid sharing it with the insects; she bit into a chocolate eclair and swallowed it whole. Then she attacked the tartlets, whose plump strawberries shone like stained glass beneath their jellied varnish. Under the pressure of her powerful jaws, the napoleon broke apart and cream spurted out in all directions, caught just in time by Estelle's tongue, which hastily scraped off the layers of puff pastry. Flakes of meringue and coconut drifted down like snow on the bib of her dress as she bolted the remaining sweets with her sharp-edged, voracious teeth.

Her mastication was interrupted by Vincent's appearance.

"Come, Mother. Come into the house. There's been an accident ..."

Before rising to her feet, she licked her fingers with a greedy growl, then wiped them on her satiated paunch.

III

BASEMENT

1962

I magine! Just a year ago the Delormes had celebrated their silver wedding anniversary with the assurance that a radiant future stretched out before them. Avoiding all expense, Louis-Dollard had given Estelle a twenty-five-cent coin wrapped in a handkerchief – the equivalent of one cent for each year of their life together. He presented her the gift as she awoke and was propping herself up on a pile of pillows. As he beheld her drooping eyelids and dishevelled hair, Louis-Dollard had to concede that his better half had offered little resistance to the implacable assault of time. For all that, she was the mother of his son, the mistress of his household, the guardian of his bank and, in this light, he was content at having chosen the best possible partner. She had proven time and time again that she was worth her weight in gold – which, in her case, amounted to something. What more could a husband ask from a wife?

Estelle was delighted by her husband's charming attentions.

"I have something for you too," she said as she withdrew a twenty-five-cent coin from the drawer of her bedside table. In her case, she had not bothered to wrap it.

That they exchanged the same gift not only brought them no end of amusement but also a healthy sigh of relief. Her Majesty forbade that one should give the other more than he received, which would have caused a disparity in their respective accounts! And so the day had begun under the best possible auspices, and Louis-Dollard, in an outpouring of enthusiasm, told Estelle that since their son had reached the age of majority some time ago, perhaps it was time to grant him a small measure of autonomy.

"Nothing too radical," he reassured her. "Just enough to give him the illusion of freedom."

Together they agreed to let him borrow the automobile once a month – a decision taken a bit too lightly, and which they would soon come to regret, for it would allow the serpent of heresy to slip into their little paradise and bring with it the direst of presages.

෨෬

When the day of the monthly outing finally arrived, Louis-Dollard led Vincent to the garage and, having given him good counsel, handed him the keys to the car – a leaf-green Dodge Regent with whitewall tires and a hood ornament representing a ram. Though it was fifteen years old, the automobile was in mint condition. Louis-Dollard bought it from a tenant who had scrupulously maintained it and had to relinquish his possession when he was transferred to Vancouver. Vincent had driven it on several occasions, when his father sent him to buy supplies at the stationer's or the locksmith's. He had ventured as far as Craig Street, to a water-pump supplier, but never deviated from the prescribed route. Today, at last, he sat behind the steering wheel of his life.

He could well have gone to the botanical gardens, or the Lachine Canal, or even the Laurentians. Instead, he headed for Rosemont to carry out the mission he had solemnly sworn he would, for now he was in a position to complete it: to find, whatever the cost, his cousin Philippe. One day when the vanilla-extract vapours had made Morula more loquacious than usual, she had given him a clue, but her directions were as brief as they were imprecise.

"Your uncle Oscar's jewellery store used to be on Masson Street, next door to a bank, if I remember correctly."

"You don't recall the address, do you?"

"I never set foot in the place."

"And his widow, what happened to her?"

"How should I know? I never met her."

"You never wondered about her?"

"Heavens, no! She was an in-law, Vincent. Why are you interested in her all of a sudden?"

"I'm curious, that's all."

The bank Morula mentioned was not difficult to locate. There was only one on the entire street, at the corner of 7th Avenue. The adjoining address no longer existed; the bank had absorbed it when it expanded. All that remained was a photo studio that had seen better days, judging by the yellowed portraits in the window. Vincent gazed vaguely at the babies with forced smiles and the young brides frozen in attitudes both awkward and rigid. He was about to turn back when the photo of a man standing in front of a jewellery store caught his eye, and the name in the window hit him like an electric shock. Without knocking, he strode into the photo studio and, begging the owner's pardon for his sudden entry, pointed to the portrait.

"Do you remember that man?"

"I certainly do," the photographer answered. "It's Oscar Delorme, my old neighbour. The poor guy had nothing but bad luck with his jewellery store. He went bankrupt in two years and died shortly after. I'm still here, thank God. Times are tough, but people always find a way to have their picture taken."

Vincent gazed at his uncle's face. In his melancholy features he sought some similarity with his father or his aunts, but could recognize no more than a vague family resemblance.

"Do you know what happened to his wife?"

"They threw her out onto the street, her and her baby, because she couldn't pay the rent. Such a kindly lady, reduced to such straits! I would have liked to help her, but I had my own problems back then, and I lost track of her. I ran into her some years later at Morgan's, I think. She came to greet me, and I barely recognized her, she had changed so much. Her hair was nicely fixed and she was elegantly dressed, with a hat and a half-veil, and a three-strand pearl necklace. She was holding a pretty little girl by the hand."

"A little boy, you mean to say."

"No, not at all. She remarried, you see, and by then she had a daughter. Her first-born son died the winter before."

Of all possible eventualities, the premature death of his cousin was the only one Vincent had not foreseen, and on hearing the sad news he felt a chasm opening up in his chest, filling him with vertigo, then nausea. After parting company with the photographer, he drove randomly through the city, his hands gripping the wheel, vainly trying to master the malaise that had overcome him. By the time he returned home, he realized that nothing but an irreversible and desperate act would expiate his guilt. He sought out his parents and announced, then and there, that he wished to take a vow of poverty and firmly intended to enter the Saint-Benoît-du-Lac Abbey.

The very next day, the family council gathered once more to discuss Vincent's case. Gastrula proposed that they set up an inquisitional tribunal and question the heretic. Blastula suggested that he be kept in quarantine to avoid the risk of contagion. Morula's view was that only love could return him to the straight and narrow, and that they needed to find the young man a fiancée – to which Louis-Dollard responded that the ideal candidate already existed, in the person of Geraldine, the daughter of Charles Knox. Estelle, who had long dreamed of an alliance with the owner of the four income properties on the other side of the park, nodded her head. But she feared that such a measure, radical though it was, would not be sufficient.

"Vincent is a grown man now. We cannot stop him from committing the irreparable. For safety's sake, we must urgently rewrite our wills to avoid our fortune from falling into the hands of a religious order. In the meantime, our heir must be made to face his responsibilities. I know it is risky, but in my opinion we have no choice: he must be initiated into the secrets of the Green Chamber at the earliest opportunity. And I believe this task is incumbent upon his father."

She spoke so decisively that no one dared contradict her, and Louis-Dollard assured her, wiping his brow, that he would promptly make all necessary preparations. He vanished until the supper hour, and awaited the end of the meal before putting his plan into action. Laying his napkin on the table, he got to his feet and ordered his son to follow him downstairs. He led him through the coal cellar and beckoned him into the Green Chamber. Vincent had not set foot there since the night of his ordeal. He was shocked to see that the pyramid of banknotes had more than doubled in size and was now so large its base covered almost the entire floor, leaving visitors little room to move.

"Breathe in the smell of money that pervades this place," Louis-Dollard said to Vincent. "Is there a headier perfume? It emanates as much from the walls as from the fortune piled up here, and it has impregnated all that we hold dearest."

To illustrate his words, he picked up the brick set atop the apex of the pyramid of banknotes, held it under Vincent's nose, and forced him to inhale.

"This brick is the capstone on which rests the edifice of the Family Treasury past, present, and future. I fashioned it myself from the clay of our ancestral ground. Were you to break it open, you would find at its centre the first coin earned by your grandfather, the Mother Coin, from which all our riches have flowed."

"I know all that," said Vincent.

His remark did not keep Louis-Dollard from telling him again that the ancient coin was a fecund womb, an unstinting genetrix endowed with magnetic powers, able to generate profit and draw capital into its orbit. Without it, their savings would vanish as through a sieve and their revenues be aborted fetuses.

"To ensure the safety of this brick, and that of the money stored here, I had the door armoured with manganese. I also equipped it with a foolproof protective apparatus. When it is closed, it displays neither knob, nor lock, nor visible hinge, because its entire locking system is built into the ceiling. Do you see those three tempered steel bars protruding from the lintel? They act as deadbolts that can be lowered from the frame and inserted in the three holes drilled in the upper crossbeam of the door, making it impossible to open. They can be opened only by a lock concealed just above us, in the living room. Now, follow me upstairs. I will show you where it is located and give you the combination."

Vincent crossed his arms, communicating his firm intention not to move a muscle.

"Is it really necessary to take me into your confidence?" he said.

"I swore to my father, on his deathbed, to look after the Mother Coin and bequeath it to my heirs."

"That combination will be of no use to me at the monastery."

"Did you ever consider that by taking Holy Orders you will be putting an end to our lineage? In the name of future generations, I beg you to reconsider your decision and allow yourself a year's reflection before you commit the irreparable. Between now and then, nothing need stop you from living in poverty if you're really intent on doing so."

Louis-Dollard's request was a reasonable one, and Vincent promised he would take it into consideration.

"One must beware of sleeping money," he told his father. "Why not use those stacks of bills to do some good?"

"I know of no better use for dollars than to accumulate them."

"Our poor house desperately needs repair," said Vincent. "Applying a coat of fresh paint, sanding the floors, replacing the kitchen tiles, and installing new windows is hardly extravagant!"

Louis-Dollard let out the same groan he did every time he had to reach for his wallet.

"Ha! It's the kind of work that will be done with your ideas and my money. This folly has already cost me an arm and a leg. There is no way I will sink so much as a red cent into it."

At that moment, I understood my venerated founder never considered me – and would never consider me – as home to a family. I had never been in his eyes anything more than a barn. A shed. A warehouse. A bank. A cash register. A vulgar piggy bank. It was useless to keep up the illusion that this unloving father would one day take care of me.

A surge of revolt made me shudder and my foundations began to shift. With the tremor, the walls of the Green Chamber cracked, and the copper coins held in place with only mucilage fell like raindrops from the vault.

"What's going on?" asked Louis-Dollard, holding fast to his brick. "Is it an earthquake?"

"The whole building is moving," said Vincent in a near-whisper, as though his voice might cause another tremor.

Louis-Dollard looked up to survey the extent of the damage, and saw that only a handful of oxidized copper coins remained attached to the ceiling. An idea was taking shape in his head, and I wondered how long he would need to understand the message I was sending him. Suddenly the truth appeared to him and his forehead broke out in a sweat.

"The coins ... they've formed letters."

"What letters?"

"Just look! There, you can see an *M*, an *A*, an *N*, an *E* ... Over there, a *T* ..."

White as a sheet, he collapsed on the pyramid of banknotes and began reciting a litany of incomprehensible words. Vincent watched, perplexed.

"I don't understand what you're trying to say. 'Manet' or something?"

"*Mane, Thecel, Phares,*" Louis-Dollard breathed. "That's what's written on the vault."

Impossible, you would have said. Yet the letters were undeniably there. Even Vincent had to agree.

"What a strange coincidence," he said.

His father almost leaped at him.

"Not a coincidence, a prophecy! It is warning me that I will suffer the same fate as Balthazar, the last King of Babylon. My days are numbered, my soul has been judged insignificant, and my legacy will be dispersed."

"Now, now. Calm down. The first thing is to repair the cracks before the walls are further damaged, then you can glue the coins back. Look after your legacy later."

Louis-Dollard brought out his trowel and brushes and got right to work. By the following week the wall had been repaired, and even a practised eye could not have detected the slightest trace of damage to the ceiling.

But my prophecy remained engraved in his memory – and I hoped with all my heart that he would remember it in terror in his final hour.

1963

L ouis-Dollard was buried this morning. With very little ceremony, I must say: no wreath atop the casket, no music during the service, no limousine, no cortège, no food served after the burial. They didn't even pin a black ribbon on my door.

At the risk of propagating suicide rumours surrounding the circumstances of his death, the Delormes buried their patriarch according to his last wishes: the members of the funeral procession could literally be counted on the fingers of one hand. Estelle led the way, sweating profusely in her beaver coat, her eyes as dry as the pine box that contained the remains of the deceased. His sisters followed, arm in arm, purloining wreaths of flowers that had been left on other graves as they walked along. Vincent trailed far behind, no doubt preferring to leave plenty of room between them. He was still shaken by his father's death, haunted by the memory of his crumpled body on the garage floor and his lips blue from carbon monoxide poisoning. The boy was devastated; not only had he been unable to revive his father to tell him the good news of his engagement, he had arrived too late to modify his will.

No sooner had they returned from the cemetery than Estelle assembled everyone in the deceased's office. She motioned them to sit down, while she took a seat in the swivel chair that had belonged to the dear departed.

"Her Majesty did not grant Louis-Dollard the grace of expiring in a state of sanctity," she said, hands folded across her ample paunch. "He died in a state of mortal sin, for there is no more scandalous waste than leaving a motor idling. It is regrettable, but there is nothing we can do. So there's no reason to delay the reading of the will."

From a folder, she withdrew the document drawn up before notary Wilfrid Labonté on September 11, 1940, number 6352 of his minutes. Morula, Gastrula, and Blastula began to squirm in their seats in eager expectation of the sizeable sum their brother had promised them in recognition of his unwavering affection, and as recompense for their deficient monthly allowance, barely enough to allow them to put some money aside. Vincent sat expressionless, as though none of this was of the slightest concern to him.

Yet he was about to inherit one of the most substantial fortunes in the Enclave, and when he finally laid hands on the fortune, he would have no alternative than to look after me. The neglect that I endured would at last be repaired, and I would soon be able to show my face to the rest of the world without shame. Farewell to the leaks, the peeling paint, the burnt-out bulbs, the cracked windowpanes, the rotten wood, and the decrepit mortar! In less than a season I would be rescued from decay and be the envy of all the houses in the neighbourhood. I even caught myself dreaming of real marble in my vestibule, hardware fashioned from polished brass, casement ceilings, mahogany woodwork, and hardwood floors. Estelle put on her glasses and began to read, and I opened the ears of my walls wide so as not to miss a single word of the last will of my negligent founder.

I, Louis-Dollard Delorme, being of sound mind and judgment, commend my soul to His Majesty and deliver myself unto his will.

To my son Vincent, issue of my union with Estelle Monet, I give and bequeath the bare ownership of the movable and immovable goods that constitute my succession, including the family dwelling.

To Estelle Monet, my beloved spouse, I give in usufruct and benefit the universality of said movable and immovable goods. Such usufruct shall cease should she contract a second marriage, or upon her decease.

To my sisters Morula, Gastrula, and Blastula, I bequeath the clothing and other personal effects with which I have so generously provided them.

Estelle cleared her throat triumphantly and opened the drawer to file away the document. The faces of the three harpies sitting in front of her lengthened and stretched to the floor, then in a single bound they leaped to their feet and stormed out of the office.

"Don't worry about your aunts," Estelle said to her son. "They'll get over it."

Such was not to be the case with me. Their indignation was nothing compared to the rage that swept over me, and owed as much to my haste as to my negligence. I had beheld the will many times over the years. Louis-Dollard used to take it from the drawer and re-examine it on his birthday. The document appeared to me complicated, tedious, and I was always content to skim hastily over the first two clauses. I felt sure that Vincent would one day inherit all property, including my person, so I stopped reading. How could I have imagined that the next clause would keep him from disposing of his fortune until Estelle had given up the ghost? So there I was, like the milkmaid in the old folk tale who is left out in the cold – and at great risk of being persecuted by our matron.

But she had other priorities for the moment, and quickly began with the most important.

"I received a call from Mr. Knox yesterday," she announced

out of the blue. "He wished to extend his condolences and, at the same time, offered to purchase our apartment building at its fair market value. As he promised to pay cash, I decided to accept his offer, providing you have no objections. The upkeep of this building is costing us more and more, and I will be relieved to not have to look after it."

Did Estelle, as usufructuary, have the right to sell real property? I am not a notary, but I had the impression her manoeuvre in no way respected the last wishes of Louis-Dollard, whose faith in the tangible value of real property was unshakable. I waited for a reaction of some kind from Vincent – the stirrings of revolt, a plea in his own defence – but he just sighed, and then spoke with a note of anxiety.

"The sale will surely produce a stack of banknotes. Where do you intend to deposit them?"

"The Green Chamber has not yet reached full capacity. There is still plenty of room for Penny's dowry, if that is what concerns you. Speaking of which, I have undertaken to draw up a marriage contract providing for communal property, which stipulates that, on your wedding day, your spouse will hand over a dowry of thirty thousand dollars to you."

Vincent didn't bother enlightening his mother by revealing the negligible sum of Penny's fortune.

"I am still sorely tried by the death of my father," he said. "It would be preferable to set this matter aside until our mourning has ended."

"Quite the contrary! Your father was deeply committed to this union, and there could be no better way to honour his memory than to proceed as quickly as possible. And need I remind you we have spent great sums of money to win Penny over to your cause? It is your filial duty to help me recover our investment. Besides, I invited your fiancée to visit us to offer her condolences, and she should be here later this afternoon. I intend to use her visit to have her sign the contract."

"You may be counting your chickens before they hatch. Penny is not as naive as you think."

"Indeed! She will quickly realize it is in her interest to combine her fortune with ours."

On that point, I could hardly contradict her. Especially when you consider that our tenant's assets amounted to no more than the five hundred dollars she owed us in unpaid rent. For her, the union would be what is called a good deal.

ༀ

When Penny finally made her appearance at four o'clock, Vincent accompanied her into the living room, where Estelle awaited them, reclining on the sofa, the back of her hand pressed against her furrowed brow. Her imitation of a grieving widow was so successful that even I was almost taken in.

"Come closer, my child, and sit down beside me," she said in her most tremulous voice. "Your presence is so comforting in this time of trial."

"My condolences, Madame Delorme. Nothing can compensate for your loss, but I nonetheless brought you some penuche, to lessen your sorrow."

Estelle sat up on her seat and a drop of saliva oozed from the corner of her mouth.

"What pleasing attention! I expected nothing less from you. You will make an excellent spouse, and my son has made an enlightened choice in asking for your hand. Your arrival in our family will benefit us immensely. All that remains is to set the date for the happy occasion. What would you say to the second of October?"

Taken by surprise, Penny glanced at Vincent. "There's no hurry as far as I'm concerned. First, we must publish the banns."

"Is that really necessary? How sad that death has cast its shadow over our rejoicing, but our lives must go on. To expedite matters, I prepared a contract. You need only sign on the bottom line."

"I would like to study it first, and seek the opinion of a notary."

"Why such precautions? Is not a good marriage founded upon trust?"

"Not blind trust."

"Between her matrimonial duties and her conjugal obligations, a newly married woman has neither time nor inclination for financial matters. Prudence requires that she assign her affairs to the capable hands of a husband who will properly supervise them."

"Will I at least be entitled to a weekly allowance?"

"You will have no need for money when you move in with us. It is understood you will be housed, fed, and your laundry looked after."

"How will I purchase clothing, toiletries, books, and other items necessary for my proper upkeep?"

"A simple requisition form will allow you to obtain a cash advance. Once it has been duly filled out and signed it must, of course, be submitted for my approval."

Penny allowed herself a few moments of reflection as she scrutinized the clock on the mantelpiece.

"Will there be a clause in the contract that provides for the cancellation of my debt to you?"

Estelle turned to her son, perplexed and disturbed.

"What debt is she talking about?"

"For several months she has neglected to pay her rent," he answered with feigned indifference.

"Your father's little indulgences are still costing us dearly, and once again, it is I who must make sacrifices to repair the damage. How much does she owe?"

"Five hundred dollars, plus interest."

Our matron attempted self-restraint, but the fury welling up in her shone through behind her honeyed words.

"My dear Penny, as you will soon bear our name I prefer

to warn you that, under no circumstances, will dishonourable debts be tolerated. You must make good on the unpaid back rent this very day, for we have an inheritance to deal with, and books to balance ..."

Penny fiddled nervously with the three strands of her pearl necklace.

"I'm afraid I'm not solvent. I don't have a penny to my name."

"Impossible! You cannot have emptied your bank account!"

"To tell the truth, it was never as full as I led Monsieur Delorme to believe. I added three zeros to the balance in my bank book to prove to him I was worthy of credit."

"Are you trying to convince me that the sales of your game brought in only thirty miserable dollars?"

"To tell you the whole truth, I had nothing to do with the invention of Safe ..."

Estelle's face quickly changed from violet to deep blue, and smoke seemed about to issue from her nostrils.

"I suppose the pearls of your necklace are fake too, you brazen fraud! You wormed your way into our family in the hope of marrying my son and living off us for the rest of your days. Well, you'll soon see what we Delormes are made of. As of today, you are expelled from your apartment and sued for forgery and fraud. The game is up, you reprobate. I'm calling the police this very minute!"

Estelle picked up the receiver and her index finger frantically began to dial.

"Wait a minute!" said Vincent. "Let's try to resolve things in a friendly fashion."

"Yes," Penny piped up. "If you send me to prison, you will never get your money back. Please allow me to make amends, and offer compensation."

Estelle stopped dialling, but did not put down the receiver.

"The compensation you are offering had better be attractive."

"I will work for you for free until I have reimbursed what I owe you, including the additional sums you have invested on my behalf. I will do the housekeeping, the laundry, the shopping, the cooking …"

The idea of having a servant on the cheap did not displease Estelle, particularly since her sisters-in-law were not as job-worthy as before. Yet she hesitated about letting the fox into the chicken coop.

"Are you ready to serve me day and night, and sleep in the basement and subsist on leftovers to keep the cost of your upkeep to a minimum?"

"Of course. I will obey you with such zeal that you will never regret your magnanimity."

"In that case, I accept your proposal."

"I will prepare to move in without further delay, which means you will not have to pay a bailiff to evict me from my lodgings."

As Penny was preparing to leave, Estelle extended her open hand.

"Not so fast, young lady! The engagement has been cancelled, so return the ring you are wearing right now."

Penny glanced at the sparkling diamonds. Instead of removing the ring from her finger, she drew back her lips and shuddered ever so slightly, then bared her teeth. I thought I heard a threatening growl issue from her throat.

Just in time, Vincent stepped between the two women, not to protect his mother, but to confront her.

"She can keep the ring," he said. "For whether you like it or not, I love her more for being poor, and I have every intention of marrying her once her debt has been reimbursed."

"Your affection is so childish. You will change your mind twenty times before the end."

Then she shoved him aside and spoke to her new servant.

"Keep your distance from my son. I forbid you to speak to him, or look at him, or breathe the same air as he does. Any infraction of this rule will mean immediate expulsion from this house."

So saying, she ordered Penny out of the room and, quite well pleased with herself, popped a piece of penuche into her mouth as a reward. A glow immediately came over her face.

"By Her Majesty!" she declared. "It tastes exactly like what Giselle used to make!"

1963

On her knees, Penny dropped the heavy brush into the bucket of soapy water and wiped her hands on her apron, then wearily pushed aside the strands of hair that had fallen into her eyes. She had spent the morning scrubbing the floor, and though she made vigorous efforts to restore it to its original lustre, the worn grey linoleum resisted, as dull as the furniture she energetically polished the day before with shoe-black. I didn't want to discourage her, but she was damaging her hands for naught: she would never be able to restore the shine to something that had never shone.

But that was what Blastula demanded of her. Like a drill sergeant she issued orders to Penny from the top of the stairs. From time to time she would descend, armed with a magnifying glass and wearing her yellow rubber gloves, and carry out a detailed inspection of the work accomplished. She prospected for dust, drawing her finger across the windowsills, between the slats of the venetian blinds, and at the backs of the drawers. She hunted down grease, thrusting a toothpick into the narrowest cavities. She stalked spiderwebs in every corner. Thank God we had no silverware to polish. Our poor scullery maid would have been unequal to the task.

At midday, Morula took command and led Penny to the laundry room, where every day she handed out a new set of instructions. Morula herself used to wash the sheets once a month, but now she insisted they be changed weekly. She expected Penny to restore shirts to their original crispness by soaking them in starch and then ironing them – inside and out. Underwear had to be soaked overnight in a solution of borax and baking soda and wrung out by hand the following day to preserve the elastic waistbands. Since it would have been indecent to expose them to neighbours on the clothesline, they were to be hung discreetly on a drying rack in the corner of the laundry room. One afternoon, Morula handed her a section of curtain bleached by sunlight.

"Re-dye this in your spare time," she said when she noticed that it was already past four o'clock. "Now get cracking! Gastrula is waiting for you in the kitchen."

Ah, meal preparation! For our new recruit, it was a particular form of training in itself. Not that the dishes on the menu called for any special expertise – quite the contrary. But the list of regulations designed to avoid wasting water, electricity, and food was so long that Penny quickly forgot half of it. It was forbidden to let the water run. The refrigerator door had to be closed five seconds after being opened. The oven could not be turned on unless there were at least three different dishes to be cooked. Vegetables were never peeled, but boiled whole, and their cooking liquid used as a base for vermicelli soup seasoned with stewed tomatoes. Meat, on the other hand, had to be carefully trimmed of its fat, which would replace lard in a variety of recipes. Cabbage heels and apple cores, along with orange peels, were transformed into ketchup or marmalade. Finely chopped radishes, strawberry tops, and celery leaves were combined to make salads as bitter as they were difficult to chew. Fish heads and innards were passed through a food mill to fashion dumplings that were quenelles in name only.

Penny's evenings were no less occupied. After doing the supper dishes, she was dispatched to the laundry room, where Estelle allowed her to set up a cot. There, she would darn socks, re-hem frayed garments, sew on buttons, repair worn carpet edges, and re-loop the wayward threads of terrycloth towels. At ten o'clock she would wash herself in the kitchen sink. Despite her great fatigue, she was in no hurry to go to bed. She forced herself to stay awake, and with the help of a faint candle, she would creep around the living room on cat feet. She stopped before the mantelpiece and examined the anniversary clock from every possible angle; she lifted the glass dome, manipulated the gears, and adjusted the hour and minute hands and the gilded spheres of the balance mechanism. Then she made her way down to what had been the coal cellar and slipped behind the heating-oil tank as far as the steel door. She ran her hand over the perimeter and tested the panel with a series of soft knocks. She stood there, examining the mysterious barrier with a perplexed look. Once when she heard someone approaching, she snuffed out her candle and quickly hid behind the tank.

"Oh, it's you!" she said, relieved to see Vincent's silhouette in the doorway. "You shouldn't be here. If your mother finds us together, I'll be fired and handed over to the authorities."

"What are you doing?"

"I'm looking for a way to open this door."

"I'd stay away if I were you."

"I know exactly what's hidden behind it, and I'm not afraid of some common strongroom."

"How did you guess? Has Aunt Morula been talking too much?"

Penny slipped out from behind the oil tank, taking care not to soil her clothes, and went to Vincent.

"I owe that information to my father, who was a cabinet maker. When this building was still under construction he was selected, among all workers, to install this door and its security apparatus."

No doubt about it, the young lady was an inexhaustible source of secrets.

"Is that so?" replied Vincent. "He should consider himself

fortunate not to have been walled up in the Green Chamber like the slaves who knew the secrets of the pyramids."

"Your father did not let him out of his sight from the beginning to the end of construction, and took infinite precautions to keep him away from the anniversary clock where the secret of the lock is hidden."

"My mother badly misjudged you after all. You are not a gold digger. You have come to rob us!"

His words held an accusation, but he seemed amused.

"It's true, my presence here is anything but innocent. But my purpose is to right a wrong, not to commit a crime."

"If your father was not fairly paid for his work, I will see that you are properly recompensed."

"He was paid in full, cash on the barrel. Perhaps not as much as he should have been, but enough."

"So what wrong could my family have possibly caused you?"

"A terrible wrong, I fear. An irreparable one. The ring you placed on my finger, you see, once belonged to my mother."

"So who are you, really?"

Penny stood on tiptoe and whispered in his ear.

"I am the daughter of Giselle Delorme."

ೞ

I was as stunned by her revelation as Vincent was. I gazed into Penny's face and compared it to my memory of her mother, and found, indeed, a distant family resemblance. For I had seen Giselle in person. It would have been some six months after Prosper's death. My construction had been almost completed; all that remained was to fit the Green Chamber with its armoured door.

How clearly I remember the day she presented herself here with a baby in her arms. How could I have forgotten? Snow had fallen and my front walk had not yet been cleared. Giselle was shivering in her threadbare cotton coat and clutched her infant so closely to her breast that you could barely hear its feeble cries. She rang the bell; by the worst possible luck, Estelle answered. Not having been invited into the vestibule, Giselle explained the reason for her call as she stood on the front step, feet in the snow and cheeks whipped by the wintry blast.

Oscar had left his family in dire straits, she explained, dependent on public assistance. Philippe was a sickly child, too weak to endure the hardships of the soup kitchen and poorly heated lodgings. He had come down with pneumonia, and in spite of her care, his fever had begun to rise. When it rains, it pours: the landlord had come knocking accompanied by a bailiff, and she had been thrown out of her apartment. The few pieces of furniture she possessed had been confiscated to reimburse her creditors.

On the street, desperate, she had been so naive as to think she could seek charity from the Delormes, and had spent her last pennies on a tram ticket. She was not asking for much, just a small loan, enough to pay the doctor.

"I doubt you will be able to reimburse me in the foreseeable future," answered Estelle, "and I may well never see my money again. However, that is a handsome diamond ring you are wearing. What use is it to you, now that your husband is no longer of this world?"

On his deathbed, Oscar had made his wife promise never to part with his ring. But how could anyone make good on her promise in such extreme penury? Giselle accepted Estelle's offer: thirty miserable dollars in exchange for a gem that was worth at least ten times more.

༄༅

"I have no trouble believing you," said Vincent after Penny had related the story. "To be frank, nothing about my mother surprises me anymore."

The couple sat as comfortably as possible on the narrow cot in the laundry room, in the glow from the pilot light on the water heater, while from time to time the tank gurgled faintly.

"Back then, my father was nearly forty years old and still a bachelor," Penny continued. "He never considered a change of status until he met Giselle as he was leaving this building. He found a room for her with one of his sisters, and saw that the child was given medical attention. The two of them married the next month, and I was born a few years later."

"So that's how our families' paths crossed …"

"Stories of wealthy uncles, stolen inheritances, and a hidden strongroom were the lullabies of my childhood. Often I would play a game and change the ending, I imagined Philippe turning into the avenger who would strip the Delormes of their ill-gotten gains and force them to end their days in penury. My brother would never have done such a thing – he was as gentle as a lamb. In any case, he wouldn't have had the strength: he had been saved *in extremis* from infantile pneumonia, but it weakened his constitution, and he spent most of his days confined to his bed."

"I learned I had a cousin only last year, and discovered how mother had cheated him out of his inheritance. I tried to find him and offer reparation, but I was told he was dead."

"He died after a relapse at age twelve. I swore on his grave that I would do everything possible so that those who had dishonestly acquired his rightful share would not profit from it. Vengeance is the only reason I'm here."

Vincent took her by the waist and held her close.

"I ask nothing more than to help you," he said. "Returning the stolen inheritance is the only way to expiate our crime. Unfortunately, only my mother knows how to open the Green Chamber. Even if she were tortured, she would never reveal the secret."

"That's too bad. I turned the spring of the clock and its hands in every direction and got no reaction – not the slightest click. I am just about to admit defeat."

"Meet me in the living room tomorrow night, at eleven o'clock. Together we will search for the solution. You and I can surely figure out the combination."

ಬಲ

As they tenderly bid each other goodbye at the foot of the stairs, I took comfort in the idea that I now had two allies. I had a premonition that Estelle's reign was drawing to its close. But vigilance was essential, for the old lady was suspicious, not to mention a light sleeper.

She heard Vincent cross the first floor and on his way up to his bedroom she intercepted him on the landing.

"Why are you walking around in the middle of the night?"

With a presence of mind I envied, he answered with perfect innocence that he had been awakened by a strange noise and had gone to check if the front door was properly locked.

"We are perfectly safe," he added. "You can return to bed and sleep in peace."

But Estelle's sleep was troubled. She twisted and turned into the wee hours, and her old mattress sank deeper beneath her weight.

The dark seed Vincent had unwittingly planted in his mother's mind was to make our lives considerably more complicated.

1963

This morning I felt as though I'd faced a firing squad. New holes had been drilled in all ten of my doors, inside and out, and they would soon be fitted with new locks, each of which would have its own key. Those ten keys would be added to the sixty-seven others that weighed down the key ring of our jailer-in-chief, as I call Estelle.

For fear of awakening the malevolent curiosity of the locksmiths, who were all in cahoots with burglars, she entrusted the job to Vincent and supervised every step in its execution. She then ordered him to cut down all the shrubs in the garden and fell the Manitoba maple that lent me shade, in the event a gang of thieves might be tempted to hide out in it.

The sale of our apartment building made the reinforcement of these protective measures necessary, since the fabulous sum of the transaction (settled in hard cash) had been added to the Treasury in the Green Chamber. Since then, Estelle's suspicion of the letter carrier, the meter reader, the election-handbill distributors, deliverymen, Jehovah's Witnesses, and anyone else ill advised enough to breach my property's perimeter had reached alarming proportions. At the slightest sound, she would shout, "Stop, thief!" and clutch her key ring, prepared to protect it tooth and nail, even at the price of her life if need be.

She hoped the additional locks would bring her a sense of security, but I had my doubts. Not only did she distrust Penny, she suspected Morula, Gastrula, and Blastula of plotting behind

179

her back to lay hands on her money. The three sisters-in-law had never concealed their resentment at having been excluded from Louis-Dollard's will: what if they could find a way into the Green Chamber? Perhaps she should keep them out of the living room and away from the anniversary clock?

Only Vincent continued to enjoy her confidence – but even then, when she handed him the new set of keys, she wondered if he would not make duplicates for himself ... Then suddenly an idea came to her with perfect clarity: all the locks in the world could never replace the vigilant instincts of a watchdog. And who was better placed than her to play the Cerberus?

After supper, as Penny was serving them a cup of hot water in the living room, she explained her new plan to her son.

"Tomorrow, at the crack of dawn, you will bring my bed downstairs and set it up in front of the fireplace. From now on I shall sleep in this room, and no one will be able to enter without my express permission."

Vincent restrained himself from throwing a worried look at his accomplice. If Estelle forbade access to the clock after this evening, they would never have another chance to discover the Green Chamber's combination. And despite their repeated attempts previous nights, they were no closer to their goal. The door remained obstinately shut and the loot beyond their grasp.

Estelle was so pleased by her decision that she allowed herself a small treat. She sent Penny to bring molasses from the kitchen, then opened the side door to the mahogany veneer secretary and removed the jar of Postum from its secret compartment. At the sight, the three sisters began to squirm in their seats, rubbing their hands together. Their parasitical greed visibly irritated Estelle, who proved even more parsimonious than usual in preparing their beverages and was in no hurry to recite the ritual verses to which she added a personal touch:

"What is that chime?"
"It's Postum time."
"And who shall prepare?"
"Mother Delorme with her care."
"What is her secret?"
"Stir six to the right, three to the left, five to the right, two to the left."
"And who knows the secret?"
"The golden globes that keep it."
"And who shall reap the pleasure?"
"The heir to the treasure."

Vincent watched her slowly turn her little spoon in the cups, alternating clockwise and counter-clockwise directions as prescribed by the formula: six times, then three, then five, then two. The capricious rotations of her spoon suddenly awakened an incongruous image. They made him think – he knew not why – of the oscillations of a metal detector that had just located, beneath the earth's surface, the resonances of gold. Or of treasure.

When Estelle finally passed around the cups, the Postum was almost cold. Vincent could not have cared less. He knew he had resolved the combination.

ൟ

It was eleven o'clock. Upstairs, Morula, Gastrula, and Blastula were sound asleep. Estelle had finally drifted off, exhausted, her head resting atop her pillows.

Penny joined Vincent in the living room. Rolling up his sleeves like a prestidigitator about to pull a rabbit from his hat, Vincent lifted the glass dome from the clock and set it on the mantelpiece.

"I believe my parents' ritual incantation was meant to be a reminder," he said. "I'm certain the opening mechanism is not activated by the hands of the clock, but by the four gold balls of the torsion pendulum. I'm dead certain."

With his index finger, he urged the gilded spheres in a clockwise motion until the pendulum had completed six revolutions around the axis formed by its torsion spring. He continued the same procedure following to the letter the directives of the ceremonial instructions: three to the left, five to the right, two in reverse.

As soon as he completed the manoeuvre, from beneath the floor, the muffled sound of a lock being opened could be heard. Penny threw her arms around Vincent's neck, whispered his name, and kissed him with all her might.

"Hurry! Let's get it over with!" she added. "Time is money ..."

They hurried down to the basement, lighting a candle to see their way. Holding their breath they passed through the furnace room and came to a stop, trembling, in front of the wide-open door, as if they were about to enter a new universe. Vincent took Penny's hand and together they stepped into the Green Chamber.

In the flickering light of the candle, the walls were even gloomier and the coins on the ceiling gleamed with a sickly glow. Even the portrait of Her reigning Majesty, our good Queen Elizabeth II, seemed strangely sinister. The pungent smell of calcined chromium oxide caught in their throats, and Penny needed a few moments to take in the bundles of banknotes stacked up with geometric precision before letting out a long whistle.

"Are you really sure you want to give up all this?" she asked. "You could keep some of it ..."

With an angry kick, Vincent sent a flight of bills fluttering into the air.

"This money is as poisonous as the verdigris that corrodes this vault. If I touch a single dollar, my soul will be sullied by its corruption, and I would not resist the temptation to hang on to the entire fortune."

"Why not give it to charity?"

"Maybe, in other circumstances, banknotes are just harmless

paper, a simple medium of exchange between two parties to an honest transaction. Not these. They've been stored so long in this room that they've absorbed the Delormes' perverted sense of economy, their avarice, their taste for filthy lucre, their greed. By sitting here unused, they have taken on such inertia that they resist any attempt to spend them, and when you touch them, you are overwhelmed by the need to accumulate and hoard them. Not even the best intentions in the world could change their profoundly evil nature."

"Those are my thoughts as well," nodded Penny in approval. "We have no choice: we must destroy them, down to the very last bill."

At first I thought she was joking, but the couple's solemn expression left no doubt as to their determination. Before I could do a thing to stop them, they each dropped their candle onto the stacks of banknotes and stepped back to safety. The bills caught slowly at first. Soon tongues of bright green flame flared up and consumed the entire treasure with a powerful suction sound. The smoke from the blaze was thick and black, coating the sad portrait of King George VI with soot. In a phosphorescent green shroud, the Green Chamber was transformed into a funeral pyre as its contents burned and crackled like shattered glass. The blaze made me fear that my entire structure might be consumed, but it remained confined to the thick walls of the former coal cellar and gradually died down as the banknotes were consumed. Soon I could barely feel the venomous heat radiating.

Penny and Vincent retreated into the furnace room, coughing. They both seemed greatly relieved.

"Justice has been done, has it not?" said Penny.

"My mother won't see it that way. She'll certainly try to have us thrown in prison."

"We best clear out."

"I don't intend to stay here a minute more. My suitcase is waiting in the vestibule. And yours?"

"I just have to lock it. Where will we go?"

"Out of the Enclave, for starters. Then we'll see."

In the treasury there had been enough money to build a house twenty times larger than me, and I had to accept, painfully, that I would be neither maintained nor repaired nor restored anytime soon. And yet I felt I had been relieved of a great weight – as though the banknotes were the gangrene that led to my decrepitude, and their incineration purified me. For me, as for Vincent and Penny, it was the day of my liberation. But before taking final leave of the Green Chamber that bound me to the past, I had one last account to settle, a final victim to immolate.

೨೮

By the time the smoke reached the upstairs, Penny and Vincent had long fled. They didn't even bid me farewell. But I don't hold it against them for abandoning me: it was in the order of things. They are young; they have their own lives to live – not the life the family set before them. I only regret they could not witness the spectacle that was about to take place.

The acrid stench soon awakened Estelle, who leaped to her feet and called out to Vincent for help. When he did not respond, she rushed into his room and saw the empty shelves, the rolled-up carpet, the mattress folded over. She immediately understood that something terrible had happened.

She rushed down to the living room and saw that the glass dome was not in its spot on top of the clock. She ran every which way, shaking the keys on her ring like a leper his bell. Had she intuited that her fortune had gone up in smoke, and that she would soon join the ranks of the penniless? As she passed by the laundry room, she noticed that Penny was not there, and cursed herself for letting the woman insinuate herself into the house. She hurried into the coal cellar, though by now she knew what lay in store for her, for she had detected the smell of money through the clouds of smoke.

The bellowing of a slaughtered animal: that was her cry of despair as she laid eyes on the last flickering embers on the floor of the Green Chamber. It was too late to save a single bill, but even though she burned her hands, it did not stop our matron from rummaging through the remains of her twenty-six years of patient saving, shameless theft, extortion and misuse of funds, of cupidity of the most vicious kind. Of the mass of banknotes there remained only a thick layer of flaky ash, greasy with soot, which soon blended with the spittle that pooled at the corner of Estelle's mouth and trickled down her chin in fine black filaments. I must confess: I felt relieved to see her crawl that way, lost without the compass that had given her life its sole direction.

Now she was rolling in the ashes, imploring His Majesty for pity, like a sinner in search of absolution, unable to escape punishment. But she was not yet prepared to admit defeat. Just when I thought she was totally devastated, she pulled herself up with a triumphant cry. In the dying light of the fire, her hand fell upon the brick containing the Mother Coin, and she brandished it like a holy relic before the soot-stained portrait of His Majesty.

"All is not lost," she cried out to the effigy of the King. "Our fortune can rise once more from the ashes!"

I had overlooked the foundation stone upon which I had been built, and which underlay the crimes of the Delorme family. Through the power of the Mother Coin, Estelle could recover the strength to rebuild her fortune, one penny at a time. I couldn't let her out of here – I knew what I had to do to settle my score with her once and for all.

ന്ധ

A draft of air was sufficient for the door to the Green Chamber to slam shut. Upon impact, the deadbolts engaged and the room was perfectly sealed. In this closed space where the oxygen had been burned away by the fire, how long could someone survive?

An hour? Two? Maybe longer by keeping still and breathing as shallowly as possible. But Estelle began hammering on the door with both fists, shouting the names of her sisters-in-law, commanding them between coughing fits to free her. But had the three sisters heard her, I doubt they would have lifted a finger to help.

Estelle was gasping for breath, and her legs would not support her. She collapsed into the ashes with the determination of someone who would not be getting up again. As she fell, she closed her fingers around the brick and tried to crack it open with the little energy she had. The brick crumbled slightly at the corners, but its heart held firm. Like the Delormes, it would not hand over its fortune so easily. In desperation, Estelle brought it to her mouth. She opened her jaws wide and attempted to bite through it. Her incisors shattered on the brick with a noise that shocked my ears.

"I might die here, but no one can stop me from taking my money to paradise," she howled through bleeding gums.

She managed to break off a section of fired clay. Encouraged, she worked more furiously, gnawing away like a jackal on carrion. Did she really believe that by swallowing the Mother Coin she could keep it in her black soul? She would need much more than that to pay nature its due. If there were divine justice, Estelle would soon be carried to another green chamber, not much different from this one, lit by the flames of hell. There she would be condemned to look on as her money burned for all eternity, until the end of time.

EPILOGUE

1964

The bailiffs quickly brought their macabre discovery to the attention of the authorities. It was not long before police cars appeared, sirens wailing, closely followed by the van from the morgue with the coroner aboard. The investigators visited every room to make sure no other skeletons were hiding in my closets. They found nothing but clues to the lives of dissolution that Morula, Gastrula, and Blastula had been leading since that morning when, understanding that Estelle was no longer there to regiment them, they felt able, at last, to give free rein to their natural penchants. In a jerry-rigged alembic, the eldest concocted adulterated essence of vanilla, the second burned excess calories by smoking cigarettes, while the youngest spent hours in the bath caring for her skin lesions.

What a wild life they led for an entire year! As if returning to childhood, they braided and beribboned each other's hair, quarrelled ceaselessly, challenged one another with impossible dares, played infantile practical jokes. No one was there to impose a curfew, so they stayed up all night and often went to bed at dawn. And when they finally fell asleep, they would frequently spend a whole day in that pursuit. It wasn't long before they stopped bothering to get dressed, and they lived in their housecoats. They never uttered the names of Estelle, Louis-Dollard, and Vincent. But they often spoke of "Papa" and always praised him for his foresight, which made it possible for them to live a life of ease.

Since they had always been kept away from managing the

household, what could they have known about the financial obligations that entailed? It never occurred to them to wonder how they would pay the grocery bills once the petty cash had been exhausted. They believed that water, electricity, heating, and city services were provided free by the Enclave. When the electricity was disconnected, they used candles for light. When heating-oil deliveries were suspended, they burned the cupboard doors for heat. In the vestibule the bailiffs found a veritable mountain of unopened mail: bills to be paid, disconnection notices, lawyers' letters, court summonses ... The three sisters never suspected that the receiver general, acting in the name of Her Majesty, had examined Louis-Dollard's income tax report and levied a tax against his estate, demanding prompt and immediate payment of it, failing which a notice of expulsion would follow.

෨෬

As the ambulance attendants were wrapping Estelle's remains in a shroud and carrying them away on a stretcher, the neighbours came onto their front porches and observed the comings and goings of the police with a mixture of curiosity and indignation. Never had such a scandal disturbed the peace and quiet of the Enclave. As recently as yesterday, the unwelcome attention would have thrown me into distress, and I would have been mortified to see my reputation so irremediably stained. No longer. For the first time in my life I felt not the slightest shame, no fear of what people might think of me. What did it matter if I was to be associated with a sordid tragedy? From my full two storeys, I looked down scornfully upon he who would dare cast the first brick.

I imagined that after the police had departed, the bailiffs would send in their movers. The brutes would take away the leather sofa, Estelle's bed, Louis-Dollard's desk, the desk with the secret compartment, and the anniversary clock. The car in which my venerated founder met his death would be dispatched to the wrecker's. The portrait of His Majesty George VI and the brick that held the Mother Coin would be consigned to the refuse heap.

I could already feel a sense of emptiness, of nakedness, of dispossession. My rooms spoke in the echoes of the voices that once inhabited me. A chapter of my history had come to an end, but the story itself was far from over. Soon, another family will take up residence, a family that will have heard nothing of the Delormes and that will have no interest in the origins of the Enclave. They will no doubt be nouveaux riches intent on impressing the neighbours and will undertake major renovations. I will have a new kitchen, a modern bathroom, a colour television set. I could imagine the care that will be lavished upon me, and the rich fabrics and fine wood that will decorate me. I will host children's birthday parties and receptions. At Christmastime my façade will be illuminated, and come summer, my flower beds will bloom ... At last, the Green Chamber will be forever sealed and, with it, all my memories and all my secrets.

I have not given up the hope of seeing Vincent again one day. He will return to visit the Enclave with Penny. They will have married. They will have a family. They will have six children and want to show them where everything began. But a house has no soul other than that of its occupants, and they will barely recognize me. I will have become a stranger to them. It will seem as though they had never lived here.

What more could I possibly wish them?

AUTHOR'S ACKNOWLEDGMENTS

To Antoine Tanguay, who sent me off to my room to think things through, and without whom I would never have come out again.

To Chloé Legault, Tania Massault, and Hugues Skene, who worked with the inexhaustible energy of an anniversary clock, and who know all the secrets of Éditions Alto's combinations.

To Claude Aubin, who swept clean the Delorme house, and Julie Robert, who handled the household chores with the powerful efficiency of Cuticura soap.

To the penuche of my friends: Michèle Mayrand, Gilles Jobidon, Mathieu Langlois-Larivière, Jean-Philippe Chénier, David Dorais, Isabelle Grégoire, Marc Gamelin, Ihosvany Hernández González.

To my loyal translators, Fred A. Reed and David Homel, who were not afraid to spend months locked up in the Delorme house.

To Kevin Williams, Charles Simard, and all the wonderful people at Talonbooks, for their enthusiasm and many kindnesses.

To my treasures Catherine, Étienne, Mathieu, and Mathilde, not to mention Winnie, the fox terrier that guards my computer.

To Jean-Claude, for the shared words and promises kept.

And to Serge, who is always present.

ABOUT THE TRANSLATORS

A three-time winner of the Governor General's Literary Award for French-to-English Translation, plus a nomination in 2009 for his translation of Thierry Hentsch's *Le temps aboli* (*Empire of Desire: The Abolition of Time*), **Fred A. Reed** has translated works by many of Quebec's leading authors, several in collaboration with novelist David Homel, as well as by Nikos Kazantzakis and other modern Greek writers. Reed worked with documentarist Jean-Daniel Lafond on two documentary films: *Salam Iran: A Persian Letter* (2002) and *American Fugitive: The Truth About Hassan* (2006). The two later collaborated on *Conversations in Tehran* (Talonbooks, 2006). His latest work is *Then We Were One: Fragments of Two Lives*, published in 2011 by Talonbooks. Reed resides in Montreal.

ABOUT THE AUTHOR

Martine Desjardins was born in Town of Mount Royal, Quebec, in 1957. The second child of six, she started writing short stories when she was seventeen. After receiving a bachelor's degree in Russian and Italian studies at the Université de Montréal, she went on to complete a master's degree in comparative literature, exploring humour in Dostoevsky's *The Devils*. She worked as an assistant editor-in-chief at *ELLE Québec* magazine and, for ten years, was a book reviewer for *L'actualité*, an award-winning French-language current affairs magazine in Canada.

Her first novel, *Le cercle de Clara* (*Fairy Ring*), was nominated for the Prix littéraire du Québec in 1998. She was awarded the Prix Ringuet for *L'évocation* (*A Covenant of Salt*) in 2006, and the Sunburst Award for Excellence in Canadian Literature of the Fantastic for *Maleficium* in 2013. She received the Prix Jacques-Brossard de la science-fiction et du fantastique for *Maleficium* in 2010, and again for *La chambre verte* (*The Green Chamber*) in 2017.

Desjardins currently lives in Town of Mount Royal with her fox terrier Winnie.

PHOTO BY JULIE ARTACHO